D0044525

Wish on All the Stars

Wish on All the Stars

BY LISA SCHROEDER

SCHOLASTIC PRESS | NEW YORK

All rights reserved. Published by Scholastic Press, an imprint of Scholastic Inc., *Publishers since 1920.* SCHOLASTIC, SCHOLASTIC PRESS, and associated logos are trademarks and/or registered trademarks of Scholastic Inc.

The publisher does not have any control over and does not assume any responsibility for author or third-party websites or their content.

Library of Congress Cataloging-in-Publication Data available
ISBN 978-1-338-19577-4

10 9 8 7 6 5 4 3 2 1   19 20 21 22 23
Printed in the U.S.A. 37
First edition, July 2019
Book design by Yaffa Jaskoll

For all the kind and compassionate helpers in the world. Thank you.

Wish on All the Stars

One

A SPECIAL GIFT

Emma pulled a small red gift bag splattered with blue and gold stars out of her backpack. "I got you guys something," she told us, her green eyes twinkling like stars as she smiled.

Carmen beamed. "My very own squirrel monkey? Oh, Emma. You shouldn't have!"

"Why, what a good guess, a squirrel monkey that could fit inside a seashell," Emma joked.

I gasped. "A miniature monkey! Wouldn't that be cool?"

"They'd become the most popular pet, for sure," Emma said.

"Hey, you know what?" I said. "We should go to the San Diego Zoo sometime and check out the monkeys together. The zoo I went to a lot in Bakersfield, where my dad works, is only for animals native to California."

"So, no monkeys?" Carmen said. "That's sad."

"Totally sad," I replied.

1

"But now that we've been talking about it," Carmen said, "I don't want to just visit monkeys, I want my very own to take home."

Emma held out her hands like a referee. "Okay, guys, sorry to tell you, but I didn't get you tiny squirrel monkeys. Any other guesses?"

I stared at the bag, wondering what it could be. We'd quickly eaten our lunches and then asked for passes to the library so we could have our first official meeting of the Starry Beach Club. Just five days before, we'd finally met Carmen, the girl who'd responded to my letter after Emma and I tossed bottles containing secret messages into the sea. My bottle apparently washed ashore as soon as we left, and Carmen, who'd been building a sand castle with her brother, couldn't resist. She'd grabbed the bottle, read the letter, then sent me an email that said, among other things, *Do you really want to be a part of something special? Because I have an idea. I wish on stars all the time. I bet you do, too. And I was thinking about all the other people like us. Sometimes their wishes come true, but sometimes they don't. Maybe the stars need helpers now and then. So let's help. Maybe we could call ourselves the Starry Beach Club . . .*

She'd told me to find someone's wish and make it come true, then signed her email as "Some Kid at the Beach." Finding a good wish and making it come true wasn't as easy as it might sound. But finally, Emma and I made something wonderful happen for our kind old neighbor, Mr. Dooney.

Now, with Carmen's help, it was time to move on to our next wish-granting project: saving our town's bookmobile.

"Okay, here's a guess," I said. "You found a nice, big parking space for the bookmobile."

Carmen chimed in. "One with a beautiful view of the ocean for Mr. and Mrs. Button."

"Mrs. Button can write in her notebook of beautiful things," I continued, "while watching the magical surf hit the sand."

Emma stuck her bottom lip out for a second before she replied, "If only."

The bookmobile, along with the people who ran it, Mr. and Mrs. Button, had become one of the best parts about moving to Mission Beach from my hometown of Bakersfield. But last week we'd learned that the new manager of the grocery store where the Buttons parked the bookmobile wouldn't allow them to stay for free anymore. They'd have to start paying rent or leave.

I gave Emma's arm a squeeze. "Sorry. Didn't mean to make you feel bad. Can we just open the gift, please? I'm dying to know!"

She reached into the bag and pulled out three little boxes wrapped in baby-blue tissue paper. "One for you, Juliet," she said, pushing one toward me. "One for you, Carmen. And one for me."

"I love that you wrapped one for yourself, even though you know what it is," Carmen said.

"Would've ruined the surprise if I didn't," she said. "Okay, on the count of three, let's open them. One. Two. Three."

I carefully tore the tissue paper while Carmen and Emma ripped theirs open like little kids on Christmas morning.

"Oh, Emma, it's so cute," Carmen squealed. I stayed focused on my own box so I wouldn't have the surprise ruined.

"I'm so glad you like it, even if it's not a miniature squirrel monkey. Meanwhile, I guess Juliet's going to save the three inches of paper and reuse it," Emma teased.

I opened my box. Inside was a teensy-tiny bottle with a note rolled up inside it. I picked up the bottle and saw that it hung on a pretty silver chain. "Oh my gosh," I said. "It's perfect! Where'd you find these?"

"Molly helped me order them from Etsy," she said. "It's a website where people sell things they've made. In case you were wondering why I kept putting off our first official meeting, this is why. I wanted to wait until they came in the mail."

As we all went to work attaching them around our necks, I asked, "Did you write us notes on the tiny pieces of paper using your best tiny handwriting?"

"No, but you can pretend I did," she replied.

"What would you have written?" Carmen asked.

"Um . . ." She thought for a moment. "I would have said,

4

'Always remember, wishes do come true.'" Then, in almost a whisper, because we were in the library after all, she started singing, *"When you wish upon a star . . ."*

I joined in, quietly, on the next line.

"Is that from a movie?" Carmen asked.

Emma often broke into song during conversations and I was totally used to it by now. Even loved it, actually. Carmen, however, still seemed a little surprised by it.

"Yes," I said. *"Pinocchio.* I think. Is that right, Emma?"

"That would be correct," she replied.

"Oh, okay," Carmen said. "I don't think I've seen that one."

"It's really good," Emma said. "Your little brother would probably like it. And you, too, of course. I have the DVD at home if you want to borrow it. Our family loves movies, especially Disney ones. Does your family watch movies very often?"

She shrugged. "Yeah. I guess. Anyway, are we going to get to our official business? If we don't hurry, the bell's gonna ring."

This was what usually happened when we asked Carmen something about her family—she changed the subject. She was so different from how Emma had been when I'd first met her. Emma and I had hit it off right away. And when she'd introduced me to her big family and shown me their cute ice cream shop, the Frozen Spoon, I'd liked her even more. I definitely liked Carmen, too, but I was still getting to know her, and it seemed like there was a lot I didn't know.

I thought of my own family situation and how, at first, I hadn't wanted to tell Emma that my parents were separated. Maybe Carmen had something she was nervous about telling us. Maybe she just needed a little more time to get to know us and to see that we would never say or do anything to hurt her. All I knew was that I really wanted to prove to her she could trust me.

Things I know about Carmen

* *She lives with her mom and her eight-year-old brother, Oscar.*
* *She's never mentioned her dad, so I don't know anything about him.*
* *She builds incredible sand castles.*
* *She loves Vincent van Gogh and his artwork, just like I do.*
* *She walks to school from her apartment while Emma and I have to ride the bus.*
* *Her mom is from Guatemala and she told us her mom makes the best chiles rellenos in the world.*
* *She doesn't like to swim in the ocean because she's afraid of sharks.*
* *When I told her I have a cat named Casper, she said she couldn't wait to meet him and that she's wanted a cat for as long as she can remember. Her mom has always said no.*
* *She loves monkeys, especially the very cute squirrel monkey.*
* *She's Starry Beach Club Member #1 and I like her a lot.*

Two

PLAN IN PLACE

I looked at the clock on the wall above the door of the library. We had five more minutes until lunch was over.

"What do you guys think we should do?" I asked as I fished the Tic Tacs out of my pocket and passed them around to my friends. "To save the bookmobile?"

Emma popped one in her mouth before she leaned in. "I think we basically have two choices: We can either figure out a way to convince the manager to let the Buttons stay for free or try to raise money to pay the rent."

"He should let them stay for free," I said. "I bet he hasn't even thought about the fact that it's good for business. Don't you think that sometimes people stop in at the little library and then decide they might as well run into the store for groceries, too?"

Carmen's fingers fiddled with her new necklace.

"Especially when the bakery is making something that smells delicious."

"Maybe that's what we should do first," Emma said. "We should try to convince the new manager to let the book-mobile stay for free."

"And how do we do that, exactly?" I asked.

"We could go and talk to him," Carmen said.

"I'm afraid he'd take one look at us, see that we're kids, and laugh in our faces," I said. "I mean, do you really think he'd take us seriously?"

Carmen shrugged. "We won't know until we try."

We were quiet for a minute, lost in our own thoughts. As I put the mints back in my pocket, I tried to imagine the three of us going into the store and asking to speak to the manager. "Why?" the clerk would ask. "You girls have some bubble gum you'd like to return? Didn't like the flavor or did it turn your teeth blue? I'm sorry, kiddos, but we have a no-return policy on bubble gum."

Just thinking about walking in there and asking for the manager made me feel woozy.

"Carmen's right," Emma said. "We need to at least try."

"What will we say?" I asked.

Emma cleared her throat. "Hello, Mr. Manager." She leaned in and whispered, "We wouldn't call him Mr. Manager, though. We'd call him by his name." She sat up straight and continued in her most serious voice, "The three of us would like to urge you to allow the bookmobile to remain on your property for free. It's good for the community, it's good for your business, and it's good for kids like us because it helps keep us out of trouble."

"We're such troublemakers," I joked. "Trying to make people's wishes come true is such a horrible thing to do."

"Can we tell him it makes him look like a jerk if he forces them to move?" Carmen asked.

"Hm," Emma said, tucking her wavy blond hair behind her ear. "I don't think calling him names would be a good move. We need to . . ."

Her voice trailed off, like she was looking for the right word.

"Kill him with kindness?" I asked. "That's something my mom likes to say."

"I've never heard that," Carmen said. "What does it mean?"

"It means that sometimes a person expects you to be mean and angry," I explained. "But instead, you do the opposite, and you're so sickly sweet, it's like this huge surprise and it usually works some kind of magic and you get what you want."

"I love that," Emma said. "Yes. That's what we'll do. We'll be so kind, he won't know what hit him and he'll tell us that *of course* the bookmobile can stay at no cost."

"Maybe he'll even throw in a year's supply of cookies from the bakery," I said. "The gooey fudge ones they sell there. Mmmm, they're so good. Thanks a lot, friends. Now I'll be dreaming of those cookies for the rest of the day."

"Welp, now we know what Juliet's biggest wish is," Emma said. "All the fudge cookies she can eat."

We all laughed, and then the bell rang. We stood up and grabbed our backpacks. "When should we do it?" Carmen asked. "Go and see the manager, I mean?"

"What about after school today?" I asked.

"I can't," Emma said. "I have to help at the ice cream shop after school."

"Tomorrow?" Carmen suggested.

"I'm going to my dad's for the weekend and I'm leaving right after school," I said as we moved toward the door. "So I guess that leaves us with Monday."

"Monday it is," Emma said. "That'll give me time to practice being kind and convincing at the same time."

"Do you want me or Juliet to come up with something to say?" Carmen asked.

I liked that she was asking this question. She wanted to make sure we were all doing everything we could to help Mr. and Mrs. Button. Emma was probably the most confident of the three of us, but maybe there was something we could come up with so Emma didn't have to do all the work. Also, wouldn't it look funny if there were three of us there but only one of us was speaking?

"Maybe you can brainstorm other reasons why the bookmobile should be allowed to stay for free," Emma said.

"The more reasons we have, the harder it will be for him to refuse, right?"

I looked at Carmen and she nodded. "Yeah, we can do that," I said.

"Okay, see you guys later," Carmen said as she gave a little wave.

"See ya!" Emma said while I waved back.

"I wish she had P.E. with us," I said as walked toward the locker room.

"Same."

"Have you noticed that she doesn't really like talking about herself?" I asked.

"What do you mean?"

"It seems like every time we ask her something about her life or her family, she kind of . . . changes the subject? Like, when you asked her if her family watches movies very often."

Emma shrugged as she dropped her backpack on the bench next to our lockers. A couple of other girls came in, talking and laughing. "She told us they did, didn't she?"

I looked at the girls and knew this wasn't really the right time to talk about this.

"I just hope . . ."

"What?" Emma asked.

"I hope she knows she can trust us. That's all."

Emma looked like she was going to say something to

reassure me, but a bunch of other girls came in, so I moved over to my locker.

"Who's ready to play badminton?" a girl yelled.

"Stop making such a racket," another girl yelled back. "Get it? Racquet?"

A few girls groaned while others laughed.

Middle school P.E.—where one minute you're miserable and the next you're laughing at the ridiculousness of it all.

Reasons the bookmobile should stay for free

1. The bookmobile is pretty and people are drawn to pretty things.
2. Tourists need books, and if they don't remember to pack some, what are they supposed to do if there aren't any bookstores nearby?
3. Books make people happy and happy people eat more, so they'll buy more groceries?
4. ??????

(This is hard. Why isn't there an easy way to say: A good human would let them stay, so just be a good human?)

Three

WELCOME BACK, MAYBE?

Casper sat on my bed, watching me as I packed for the weekend. "I'm really sorry I can't take you with me," I told him before I leaned down and kissed the top of his soft, most kissable head. "Mom will take good care of you. Remember she's a vet, so she basically lives for animals, Casper. Like, I'm pretty sure she loves animals more than she loves her own children. So you'll be fine, all right? I promise."

He stared at me with his green eyes, his little pink nose twitching ever so slightly. He was an excellent listener and I was sure he understood everything I said. Everything!

I went to my dresser, grabbed a couple of pairs of socks, and tossed them into the suitcase. I picked up my phone to see if I'd missed a text from my Bakersfield best friend, Inca. I'd asked her when she wanted to get together, but she

15

hadn't texted me back yet. I was so excited to see her. Excited to see my dad, too. Just . . . excited!

Until Miranda came in and acted like the world was coming to a fast and furious end. My sister is the queen of ruining a perfectly good moment. It's a little like biting into a perfectly decorated cupcake and finding walnuts.

"I don't want to go," she wailed, throwing herself face-first on my bed, causing Casper to run off like a firecracker had been lit under the bed.

"Hey," I said. "That wasn't nice. And what are you talking about? We get to see Dad. Don't you want to see him?"

"I guess, but Lucy and the other girls are going for brunch on Sunday and getting pedicures and who knows what other fun things, and I'm going to miss all of it. And the bus, Pooh. We have to ride the *bus*!" She groaned. "It's so lame."

"I don't think it's going to be that bad," I told her. "Bring a book. Or sleep. Whatever. It's four hours, not four days. You'll survive."

"Do you think the bus has a way to keep our phones charged?" she asked, rolling over onto her back.

"Miranda, it's not like it's a horse and buggy," I said as I fingered clothes in my closet, trying to figure out what shirts to pack. "Pretty sure they'll have outlets at our seats."

"What are we even going to do all weekend?" she asked. "Do you think he has things planned?"

"I hope so," I said as I took a T-shirt and hoodie off their hangers. "But we can see our friends, too. What's April doing? Aren't you excited to see your best friend, even if you're not excited to see your own father?"

"She's gonna be out of town. Her whole family is going to see Bruno Mars in Vegas. Doesn't that sound fun? How come we never do fun things like that?"

"Do you even like Bruno Mars?" I asked.

Miranda got to her feet. "Is there anyone who doesn't like Bruno Mars? But that's not really the point."

"Well, who knows what Dad has planned. Maybe we're going to have the best weekend ever. Maybe we'll go horseback riding. Or zip-lining. Or he'll take us to see an amazing musical like *Wicked* or *Hamilton*! Right? It might turn out to be the best weekend of our lives. Something we'll talk about with our grandchildren years from now."

It made Miranda smile. "Grandchildren? I'd be happy just to have something awesome to post on Instagram."

"Believe, Miranda," I said, reaching out and squeezing her arms. "Believe. And your wish will come true."

Except it didn't come true. Not even close. First of all, the air conditioner on the bus went out, so it felt like we were riding through a humid swamp. Although if that had been the case, maybe I would have gotten to see some cool animals. Alligators. Monkeys. Something. Instead I just got to look at my sister, who moaned and complained the entire time.

When we finally came to our stop, all I wanted as we headed toward the doors of the bus was to breathe some fresh air and get a cold drink. At least that's what I thought I wanted, until we walked through the train station and realized our dad wasn't there to pick us up.

Miranda texted him right away. "I can't believe he's not here," she muttered.

"He probably just got stuck in traffic," I said.

"I'm starving," Miranda whined. "Aren't you starving?"

"No. I'm not. I ate a granola bar and an apple that I brought along with me, remember? But you didn't want anything, because apparently taking a granola bar from your sister's snack bag is beneath you."

"Wait. Juliet. You have an entire snack *bag*?" She reached for my backpack. "Give it to me."

"Excuse me, dear, obnoxious sister," I said, pushing her hands away. "You know in our family we say please and thank you."

"Give it to me!" she said louder as she tried to rip the backpack off my body.

I may or may not have scratched her eyes out at any moment if Dad hadn't suddenly appeared. "Girls," he said in a hushed tone. "What's going on?"

"Miranda is acting like a spoiled three-year-old because she chose not to eat on the bus, even though I offered her something," I told him.

"Why are you late, anyway?" Miranda asked.

"I'm sorry," he said as he pushed his glasses up. "Traffic was really bad and I didn't expect it to be that way. Anyway, I'm here now, so . . . can I have a hug? I've missed you two so much."

I leaned in and gave him a hug. The familiar smell of his aftershave made me feel like I was home. I'd missed that smell. When we finished, Miranda started walking toward the door that led to the parking lot. I looked at Dad and shrugged as if to say, "Whatcha gonna do?" He patted me on the back and smiled.

"Was the bus ride okay?" he asked.

"I guess," I said. "It was stuffy, though, and I drank all my water. Can we get something to drink?"

"I thought we'd pick up a pizza on the way home to have for dinner," he said. "You can choose a drink there, okay?"

"Should we call it in?" I asked.

He looked at me, confused.

"The pizza. So it's ready when we get there."

"Oh. Right. Good idea."

I pulled my phone out of my pocket. "I can do it. Are we getting it from Tony's? Hopefully?"

"Yep!"

When we walked outside, I took a deep breath. It was almost eight, so it was dark. Miranda stood waiting at the curb for Dad to lead us to his car.

"It's so good to have you girls here," Dad said, taking

my hand as he looked for cars before heading into the parking lot.

"Okay, I'm going to call and order it. What do we want?" I asked.

"Veggie for me," Miranda said.

I looked at Dad and wrinkled my nose. "How about a large half-Hawaiian and half-veggie?" he told me, knowing Hawaiian was my favorite. "I can eat either, doesn't matter to me."

After we put our bags in the trunk, Miranda got in the back seat, so I took the front. I called in the pizza and then sat back and relaxed. Now if only Inca would text me so we could make plans, life would be close to perfect. I decided to send one more:

> Hey, I'm here!!!! Going to get pizza with Dad and M. Let
> me know when we can get together.

"How's school, girls?"

Why do parents always have to ask about school? Sometimes it seems like it's all they want to talk about when it's pretty much the last thing I want to talk about. Ask me about the books I've been reading. Or what I've been painting. Or if I've eaten any good pickles lately (the answer to that will always be yes, though). Just . . . anything, Dad.

"Fine, I guess," I said.

"Miranda?" he asked, looking in his rearview.

"I passed my chemistry test," she said.

"Well, that's good news," Dad said.

I decided to change the subject. "I can't wait to see your apartment," I told him. "Do you have our rooms set up or do you need us to help with that?"

"Right," Dad said. "About that. Unfortunately, the bedroom furniture I ordered for your rooms hasn't arrived yet."

"You *ordered* furniture?" Miranda asked. "Dad, haven't you heard of IKEA?"

"I've just been so busy with work," he said with a sigh. "It seemed like the easier option."

"So what does that mean?" I asked. "Where will we sleep?"

"I borrowed some inflatable mattresses and sleeping bags from a friend," he replied. "You can pretend you're camping. Or glamping. Isn't that what they call it?"

I'd never heard of glamping. It sounded gross. Like an ugly, infected wound or something. Ew. Was he asking his children to pretend we were so severely injured that we couldn't get into a bed, so we had to sleep on the floor?

I decided I better ask. "What's glamping, exactly?"

"It stands for glamorous camping," Miranda explained. "You know, you go to an amazing place like the Grand Canyon, but you sleep in a cabin with a bed and a heater instead of sleeping in a tent on the cold, hard ground."

"Oh!" I said. "That's a lot nicer than an infected wound."

"Oh my gosh, Pooh," Miranda said. "Disgusting."

"Well, I didn't know. So, if we're pretending to camp, or glamp, I guess, can we make s'mores?" I asked.

"I have no idea how we'd make s'mores without a campfire," Dad said.

"We could look it up on this thing called the internet," Miranda said sarcastically.

"Maybe we can just buy some s'mores-flavored ice cream," I said. I didn't want Dad to have to do anything too difficult. This was our first visit since Mom, Miranda, and I had moved away to San Diego. I wanted it to go well. Better than well. It was supposed to be the best weekend ever.

"Thanks, kiddo," Dad said. "That's probably more doable."

"Will we have time to stop at the store, though?" I asked. "With everything you have planned, it's okay if we don't. When you talked about camping, it just made me think of s'mores, that's all."

"We actually, uh, need to go to the store either tonight or tomorrow," Dad said. "My fridge is pretty bare."

"Okay," I said. "It's fine, right, Miranda? We can squeeze it in with all the fun stuff we'll be doing."

Dad cleared his throat. "Um. Juliet?"

The way he said it, I knew. I knew what he was going to say next, and at the thought, it felt like my heart had dropped all the way to my toes.

"Yes?" It came out like a squeak. Which I guess makes sense because I felt about as small and unimportant as a mouse in that moment.

"I don't have much planned, except visiting the new animals at the zoo," he said. "Besides that, I thought we could watch some movies at home. Maybe bake some cookies together. It's just that I've been working—"

"So much," I interrupted. "Yeah. I know. You already said that."

"You're planning on seeing Inca, right?" he asked.

"I hope so," I muttered. Now more than ever.

Texts to Inca

* *Have you lost your phone?*
* *Did you do something so obnoxious your parents had no other choice but to take away your phone?*
* *Have you forgotten who I am? Juliet. Juliet Kelley. BFF. I think. I hope.*
* *Did you have to fly to Paris unexpectedly? If so, I hope you are having a croissant for me.*
* *If you suddenly have amnesia, I promise you want to know me. Text me back. Please? We'll get together and I'll prove it.*

Four

TEA FOR THREE

Saturday morning, as I ate a bowl of Honey Nut Cheerios, Inca finally replied.

> You're funny! Sorry, went to the Spring Fling dance last
> night. And today I'm going to Ariel's birthday party.
> Maybe tomorrow I can see you? Before you go back?

Inca went to a *dance*? That did not sound like the Inca I knew and loved. Inca was an introvert with a capital *I*. She liked staying in and watching movies or reading books, just like me. And why didn't she invite me to go to Ariel's party? Ariel and I were friends, too. We used to talk sometimes at school, and now she liked almost all of my photos on Instagram. She wouldn't mind me coming. Would she? I wanted to ask, but I was afraid. Afraid Inca would say no and then I'd feel like I was even lower on Inca's list of priorities. Like, ocean-floor bottom.

Ariel probably hadn't known I was going to be in town,

so I couldn't be upset that she didn't invite me. Still, the left-out feeling was not fun. I wanted to see everyone. Sure, moving to San Diego hadn't been too bad, since I'd met Emma on the first day and she'd made me feel so welcome. But Bakersfield had been my home forever. I missed it. And I didn't want to feel like a stranger every time I visited Dad. Like someone who was walking up to the pretty display window of Macy's and could only admire everything from the outside instead of going inside and actually shopping.

I started and erased at least ten different responses to Inca. Finally I decided to keep it simple: Okay. Our bus leaves at 2:00. Hope we can make it work!

She texted back and suggested we meet for doughnuts at our favorite doughnut shop and I was so relieved we finally had a plan. The shop was easy to get to by bus for both of us, so we didn't even have to ask our parents for a ride.

As I was putting my bowl in the dishwasher, I heard Dad's voice coming from his bedroom. The door was cracked and I wasn't trying to listen, I swear. But his apartment is about the size of our cottage on Mission Beach. That is, not very big. And just like at home, sound carried easily.

"Thought maybe we could grab dinner tomorrow night," he said in a soft, sweet voice. "I could pick you up at seven?"

There was a pause.

"No, they leave at two, so anytime after that is fine."

Another pause.

"Okay, perfect. I'll pick you up then. Look forward to seeing you, Andrea. Have a good day."

Dinner? Andrea? Was this what it sounded like? Like a man who wasn't even officially divorced yet and was dating already? When Miranda and I had thought Mom had gone out on a date, I'd gotten a funny feeling in my stomach. And now the feeling returned. It felt a little like spinning around and around on one of those old park merry-go-rounds and stopping suddenly. Dizzying.

Mom had sworn she wasn't dating yet, just going out with friends and keeping things simple, but I hadn't heard Dad's feelings on the subject at all. Well, until now. What is it that they say? Actions speak louder than words?

"Good morning, Juliet," Dad said when he appeared a minute later, the familiar smell of his aftershave filling the room. He reached for a glass in the cupboard. "You sleep okay?"

"I guess, except every time I moved, the slippery sleeping bag made an annoying sound."

"Ah yes," he said. "I know that sound well. It's all part of the camping experience."

Except we weren't camping. Not even close.

He rubbed my head as he passed by and grabbed the bottle of orange juice out of the fridge. "It'll make you appreciate your own bed tomorrow night, right?"

I was about to ask who he'd been talking to earlier when Miranda walked into the room, her hair looking like she'd had snakes sleeping in it. "You two are so noisy," she said as she stifled a yawn. She sat down at the small kitchen table and put her head in her hands. I imagined a snake slithering out onto the table and shivered.

Why was I thinking about disgusting, slimy snakes? Miranda had just opened a door and happily invited me in. This was my chance! "Yeah, Dad, I heard you on the phone earlier. Who was that? Someone named Andrea?"

Dad took another drink of his juice and set it on the counter. "Oh. Well, uh, she's someone I work with. We need to get together tomorrow and go over some things. That's all." He walked over to Miranda. "Can I get you anything to eat or drink?"

"No, thanks," she said. "I'm barely awake. The only thing I want is to go back to bed."

I looked at the clock. It was a little after nine. We had the entire day to fill. "When are we going to the zoo, Dad?"

"I thought we'd go this afternoon." He looked at Miranda. "You sure you don't want anything? Oh, you know what? I think I'll make us all some tea. How's that? I bought some at the farmers' market the last time I was there. Thought you girls might enjoy it when you came to visit."

Tea? He bought tea because he thought we *might* enjoy it? It was a little bit like me buying Casper a bag of dog treats because "well, who knows, maybe he'll like it." There were lots of things he knew for sure that we liked. Weren't there? I told myself the important thing was that he'd thought of us, even if I'd had maybe two cups of tea in my entire life.

"Miranda," Dad said as he filled the kettle with water. "Would you like to help us make some cookies to go along with the tea?"

I stared at him for a moment before I said, "Dad, you do know people don't usually have cookies for breakfast, right?"

He shrugged. "We bought the ingredients at the store last night, and you know what they say—there's no time like the present."

Miranda was like one of those dolls with eyelids that go from closed to open by simply standing the doll upright. There was no question now—she was completely awake. She hopped out of her chair and exclaimed, "It's backward day! Cookies for breakfast! I'm so on it, Dad."

"Well, in that case," I said as I went to the fridge to get my jar of pickles.

My favorite kinds of cookies

* *Homemade sugar cookies (with frosting, of course)*
* *Snickerdoodles*
* *Grandma's chocolate crinkles*
* *Frosted animal cookies (they're cute AND delicious)*
* *Chocolate chip*
* *Peanut butter*
* *Mint Oreo*

Five

A BRILLIANT IDEA

Miranda and I grew up going to the California Living Museum (also known as the CALM Zoo) as often as most kids go to the park. Since Dad worked there and sometimes needed to check on an animal over the weekend, he usually asked if Miranda and I wanted to go with him. Sometimes Miranda said yes and sometimes she said no. As for me? I always said yes. Always. I loved that place.

I have so many happy memories from the zoo.

I used to run around the big glass cage of chipmunks because that's what they did—they ran around in their cage. Their constant motion made me laugh. One time, one of them stood on a small rock and kept spinning around and around. It was hilarious. And when he eventually stopped, he turned and ran straight up one of the tree branches. I thought for sure he was going to fall off because he was dizzy, but it was no big thing.

Feeding the mountain goats was something else I loved to do when I was younger. Dad would give me a handful of food and then I'd open my palm and let the goat lick the food off with his tongue.

Miranda didn't want anything to do with that. "It's so gross," she'd said one time as the goat fed from my hand.

I'd giggled. "His tongue kind of tickles."

"Make sure you wash your hands before you even think about touching me."

Such a drama queen.

Her favorite animals at the zoo have always been the black bears. I guess they're kind of fun to look at, but I don't get the appeal. They mostly just lie around. If I had to pick a favorite, it would probably be the barn owls. They have the sweetest faces, with the shape of a heart around their eyes and beaks. Some things I learned about barn owls at the zoo: 1) Instead of hooting, they click their beaks and hiss, and 2) One barn owl can eat more than a thousand mice in a year. Amazing.

The barn owls at the zoo are the reason I started painting owls. It took me a long time, like years, to finally get to where I was happy with what my paintings looked like. I figured out the best thing to do was to keep the silhouette simple and change up the patterns and colors on the inside of the owl's face and body.

Walking through the entrance of the zoo, like I'd done at least a hundred times before, felt like coming home. If someone had asked me at that moment if I'd want to move in and live with the black bears, big cats, tortoises, owls, and goats, I probably would have said yes. There's something really comforting about going to a place that's been a big part of your life. And for the first time in a while, I didn't feel anxious about what might happen next. I didn't worry about what people might think of me. So much had changed in my life the past month, but not this. Not the zoo.

I felt like shouting out a greeting to every animal I saw, I was so happy to be back. But I wasn't five years old anymore. I needed to act like the mature eleven-year-old girl that I was. Still, when we stepped into the room with the chipmunks and no one was around, I dashed around the cage for old times' sake.

"Juliet, don't you think you're a little old for that?" Miranda asked me.

"Clearly not," Dad said with a smile.

"It doesn't feel the same," I said when I finished.

"The same as what?" Dad asked.

"The same as when I did it when I was little," I explained.

"Yep. That's growing up for you," Dad said as he put his arm around me. "Be glad you have the memories, kiddo. Come on. Let's go meet Cozy."

"Who's Cozy?" I asked.

"The new porcupine," he replied.

"That's funny," Miranda said. "Since literally nobody wants to get cozy with a porcupine."

"I'd do it!" I said. "How bad could it hurt?"

Dad grimaced. "Pretty bad, actually. No one wants to get quilled. Trust me."

"Quilled?" I asked. "Is that a real thing?"

"Definitely real," he said. "The slightest touch causes a porcupine to lodge lots of quills into the face or body of the predator. Since the quills have barbs on the ends, they're hard to get out of the skin. And painful. Just ask any dog who's ever had an unfortunate run-in with a porcupine."

"You must really love it when one gets sick," I said. "Do you have good gloves?"

It made him laugh. "Very good gloves. I appreciate your concern, Juliet."

"No problem," I said as we walked toward the porcupine exhibit. "You know I love all the animals here, but there's one I wish you had that you don't."

"And what would that be?"

"Squirrel monkeys."

"Honey, you do remember this is a zoo for animals native to California, right?"

"I know, but couldn't you make just one exception?" I asked. "They're so adorable. And everyone would want to come see them." I paused. "Wait. I know! You could change the name of the zoo from the California Living Museum to the Cute Animal Living Museum. You could still call it the CALM zoo because the letters would be the same."

"Cute Animal Living Museum?" Miranda asked. "That's kind of brilliant, actually."

"Right?" I said. "Cute animals are the ones kids want to see the most anyway."

When we got to Cozy's cage, Dad asked, "What do you think? Does Cozy make the cut for your new zoo? Is he cute enough?"

His face definitely was. "As long as he doesn't quill a poor squirrel monkey, then yes," I said. "He can stay."

"You should ask your mom to take you to the San Diego Zoo," Dad said. "Pretty sure they have them there, if I'm remembering correctly."

"Yeah, I want to go there with my two new friends," I told him. "Carmen is the one who really loves squirrel monkeys."

"You're a good friend, Juliet," Dad said.

"Get me a squirrel monkey and I'll be the most awesome friend in the world," I told him.

"Sorry, sweetie," he said. "I'm a veterinarian, not a magician."

Animals I'd want in the Cute Zoo

* Koala bears
* Giant panda bears
* Red pandas
* Red foxes
* Sea otters
* Harp seals
* Raccoons
* Bunnies
* Snowy owls
* Barn owls
* Squirrel monkeys
* Elephants (I totally think they're cute, wrinkly skin and all)

(On second thought, maybe the cute animals of the world should live in their own natural habitats whenever possible and kids like me should just watch them on YouTube.)

Six

WISHING FOR NORMAL

"Inca!" I said when she walked through the door of the doughnut shop Sunday morning. I couldn't help it—I jumped up from the table I'd snagged, scurried over, and threw my arms around her. "I'm so glad you're here."

She smirked at me. "Really? I don't know, I think you could act a little more excited, honestly."

"Ha. Very funny. Come on, let's go order. I was waiting for you."

I ordered my usual, a Boston Cream and a hot chocolate. I expected Inca to order her usual as well—a maple bar and a pint of milk—but instead she got a chocolate coconut doughnut and a latte.

"You drink coffee now?" I asked when we returned to our table with drinks and plates in hand. "When did that happen?"

She smiled. "Ariel got me hooked. At first I drank it

37

with mostly milk and a little bit of coffee. Once I got used to the taste, I moved on to a latte. Her mom has an espresso machine. It's so cool. I wish my mom were just half that amazing. The only hot drink she'll make me for me is turmeric milk. I'm so tired of drinking that." She nudged her mug toward me. "Want to try it?"

I wrinkled my nose. "No, thanks. I've tried coffee at home a couple of times. I don't like the taste. Too bitter."

After she took a sip, she said, "You need to drink it with lots of milk first, like I did. I'm so glad Ariel suggested it to me. She's smart."

I felt a little pinch in my heart at the mention of Ariel's name again as I took a bite of my doughnut. I knew I shouldn't be jealous of her, but jealousy is about as easy to control as a busy toddler. What else was Inca supposed to do, become a monk and not talk to anyone or do anything fun after I left Bakersfield? She needed friends, and if Ariel made her happy, that should have made me happy, too. I had Emma and Carmen, after all. But Inca and I had only been back together approximately six minutes and already she'd mentioned Ariel three times.

"So. Tell me. Tell me all the things." She reached back and tightened up her ponytail. One thing about Inca? She has the prettiest, waviest hair I've ever seen. It's thick and black and really beautiful. I've been envious of it forever. She gets it from her mom, who is a major health nut. Maybe

I needed to eat fewer pickles and drink more turmeric milk. Maybe that was the secret to gorgeous hair.

"We went to Dad's work yesterday and saw the new tortoise and porcupine," I told her.

"Ooh, what are their names?"

"The tortoise is named Swifty and the porcupine is named Cozy."

Inca smiled. "Someone has a sense of humor."

"I wish you could have gone with us," I said with a sigh. "It would have been so much more fun with you there. Miranda wasn't all that interested. And Dad, well . . . He seemed kind of, I don't know, distracted?"

How could I explain it? I'd thought that we were off to a good start when Miranda declared it a backward day. But Dad didn't help with the cookies at all. Miranda and I did everything, while he sat at the table, scrolling through his phone. When Miranda asked him about it, he said, "Sorry, dealing with some work stuff."

And when the cookies were finished, we asked what we should do until lunchtime. "Watch television?" he suggested.

Right. Because we traveled four hours on a bus so we could sit and watch TV? It was like he wasn't quite sure what to do with us, exactly. Or he hadn't thought through what it would really mean to spend the weekend together, just the three of us. Things hadn't been as bad at the zoo, and we'd ended up having a pretty good time. Still, I meant it when I said it would have been more fun with Inca there.

Inca didn't ask me to explain what I meant, though. Instead her phone buzzed and she kind of chuckled as she read the text, then started tapping out a reply. It seemed nosy to ask her about it, so I checked my phone, too, but I didn't have any texts. I waited for a second and then decided to send something to Emma.

> Hey. Miss you. Things are kind of strange here. It feels like I've been gone for years instead of weeks.

After that, I nibbled on my doughnut while I waited for Inca to finish.

"Sorry," she said when she set the phone down. "What were we talking about?"

"I don't know," I said, even though I totally did know. But if she didn't remember, it meant she wasn't very interested. "So, did you have fun at the dance?"

That question made her light up like a sunny day on the boardwalk. "Oh, Juliet, it was *so* fun."

"Did you dance?"

She looked at me as if I'd asked if she liked doughnuts. "Yeah. Of course. Everyone danced."

"Everyone?"

"Yeah. I mean, why would you go to a dance if you weren't gonna, you know, dance?"

"Maybe because you don't want to be the only one who stays home? Or maybe you just want to hang out with your friends." I swallowed hard. "If I'd gone I don't think I would have danced."

She took more bites of her doughnut and then wiped her mouth with her napkin, like she was really considering what to say next. "Juliet, maybe you think that now, but I bet you'd change your mind. No one cares if you look ridiculous or whatever because everyone kind of looks ridiculous, you know? That's what Ariel says. That I need to stop worrying that people will judge me because that's how you miss out on things. So that's what I did."

I couldn't deny it sounded like smart advice.

"What about you?" Inca asked. "Have you made any friends at your new school?"

Part of me wanted to tell her that yes, I had, and if it weren't for them, I'd have been totally miserable. But another part of me wanted to keep Emma and Carmen to myself. Because no matter what I said, words couldn't really describe how I felt about them and everything that had happened so far between us. Like, how awesome was it that Carmen loved Vincent van Gogh as much as I did? And then there was Emma, who had given me something I hadn't even known I'd needed—a second place to call home, with a really nice and generous family.

"Yeah," I finally said. "I've met a couple of girls." I waited to see if she'd ask me about them. Ask me how I met them or what their names were or what we liked to do together. But she didn't ask anything. She turned back to her phone and smiled. And so, I checked mine and saw I had a text from Emma.

> Sorry. Did you bring your notebook of beautiful things?
> You need to find something beautiful and write about
> it, like Mrs. Button would. I bet it'd make you feel
> better.

Maybe Ariel was smart. But so was Emma. Except, who decided it was a contest anyway?

My doughnut sat in my stomach like a brick.

"Inca?" I said.

"Yeah?" She didn't even look up.

I stood up, my legs wobbly beneath me. "I gotta go. Thanks for the doughnut date."

Now she looked at me. "Wait. Why are you going so soon? Is everything okay?"

I wanted to say *no*. I wanted to say *I miss you and I wish things were the way they were before I left and I'm sad that things between us already feel so different.* Instead I simply said, "I'm not feeling well, so I'm just going to go back to my dad's. I'm sorry. See ya later."

She kind of frowned. "Okay. I hope you feel better."

"Thanks."

Sometimes you throw a bottle into the ocean and magical things happen. And sometimes you meet up with a friend for a doughnut and everything feels wrong.

I wished it could be magical all the time, but I guess that isn't how life works.

Beautiful things in Bakersfield

* *Seeing my dad's smiling face.*
* *Tony's pizza.*
* *Sleeping bags in a warm apartment instead of in the cold and scary woods.*
* *Chocolate chip cookies fresh out of the oven with a cup of tea.*
* *A hug from Inca.*
* *Meeting Cozy and Swifty at the zoo.*
* *Getting on the bus and feeling happy about going home. A new home, but a home all the same.*

(It took me about an hour to write this list on the bus. But I did it. And it did make me feel a little better about the weekend.)

Seven

KEEPING SECRETS

I didn't tell anyone about my visit with Inca. I felt sad, but I didn't want to talk about it. It wasn't like anyone could do anything to change what happened. I'd moved away and she'd found someone to take my place. Someone way more fun than me, it seemed. The thing was, I didn't have a good reason to be upset, really. Didn't I want my best friend to be happy?

It was like my cat. I'd gone away for the weekend and it'd be horrible of me to wish that he missed me so much he sat on my bed completely miserable. No, I should hope that he and Mom were having a fabulous time eating ice cream and watching Animal Planet together.

Inca was my friend. She'd always be my friend. I knew that. But the longer we were apart, the more things would change. We'd probably keep growing more and more apart and it didn't seem like there was anything I could do about that. And it was a horrible feeling.

When I got home Sunday night, I ate dinner and went to bed. Mom asked me if everything was all right and I told her I was just really tired. Luckily, she didn't push me. Casper cuddled with me as I snuggled up in my bed with a book. Just as I was about to drift off to sleep, Miranda peeked her head in.

"Hey, can I come in?"

"I guess." As she stepped into my room, I said, "But don't bounce! Casper is comfortable."

"Okay, okay," she said as she made a point to act like I slept on a fragile sheet of glass.

"Very funny," I said. "What do you want?"

"This weekend was kind of . . . not the best," she said.

"Yeah. No zip-lining. No musical theater."

She groaned. "Pooh, the most exciting thing we did was stare at a tortoise for five minutes. I keep wondering, what happened? Is he clueless about what to do with us for two pitiful days?"

I stroked Casper's soft white body. "Mom was always the one who planned things for us to do together as a family. Movies. Hikes. Vacations. Maybe he doesn't know how to plan?"

"You know, that is really good point," Miranda said.

"Maybe he could take a class or something."

"Or . . ." She stood up and stretched. "Or it's just going to take time for him to figure it out. If only I didn't miss out on awesome stuff while that happens."

I yawned. "At least you got to spend time with *me*, right, Pooh?"

She chuckled. "Oh yeah. Absolutely." She started to head toward the door and then turned around. "Are you okay? I mean, I know it was super disappointing, but you're all right?"

I focused on Casper. His gentle purr. The curve of his tail. The arches of his adorable ears. "Yeah. I guess so. I just . . . I wish things were like they used to be," I said softly.

She stood there a minute before she finally said, "I'm sorry to say it, but you probably need to find something else to wish for." And then she left.

All day Monday, I kept checking my phone for a text from Inca, hoping she'd asked me if I felt better. Or told me she was sad we couldn't have spent more time together. Something. Anything. But nothing came. I even turned my phone off and on again, in case something might be wrong with it.

Monday after school, Carmen rode the bus home with Emma and me. We'd already decided we'd stop off at Emma's house for a quick snack and then head to the store to talk to the manager.

They asked me about my weekend but I didn't say much.

What was there to say, really? That my dad's idea of a good time was sleeping on inflatable mattresses and watching hours of *Spy in the Wild*? That it kind of felt like I didn't have a best friend anymore? That everything had changed so much in the past month I wasn't sure if I'd moved to San Diego or the moon?

As we walked to Emma's house, the sun warm on our faces, Carmen brought it up again.

"What's your dad's new place like, anyway?" she asked. "Do you have your own room?"

"I do," I told her. "He's renting a three-bedroom apartment so Miranda and I both have our own rooms when we stay there."

"That was really nice of him," Carmen said. "Did he buy you new furniture for it and everything?"

"He ordered it," I explained. "It'll probably be there next time when we visit. Would have been nice if he'd asked me what I might like, but maybe it doesn't matter that much."

"You must be excited to go back, right?" Carmen said.

The question made my head hurt. If I said yes, it would sort of be a lie. If I said no, I'd sound like the biggest jerk of a daughter ever. I glanced over at Emma. She knew from some texts that it had been a pretty disappointing weekend. Carmen didn't have a phone, so she didn't really know that things hadn't gone well. Fortunately, Emma spoke up so I didn't have to.

"Next time will be better, Juliet. New things aren't always very fun, that's all."

"I don't know," I sighed. "Right now it feels like it'll be awful forever. It's hard having parents who don't live together."

When I glanced at Carmen, she had tears in her eyes as she nodded. I didn't know if her parents were divorced or her dad had died or what. I couldn't deny I was curious, but I also knew it was best to let her tell us when she was ready.

Emma linked her arm with mine. "At least you have us, right? I know that no one can take the place of your dad, but . . ." She started singing, *"You've got a friend in me."* She corrected herself, "I mean, you've got a friend in *us*."

I smiled. "Thanks. Now, do we know what we're going to say when we walk into the store and ask to speak to the manager?"

"You're doing all the talking, right, Emma?" Carmen asked, sounding nervous.

"Did either of you come up with some totally convincing reasons the bookmobile should be allowed to stay without paying rent?" Emma asked.

"I tried," I told her. "But it's hard. It's like trying to convince someone we should take care of hungry children. Why can't everyone just think of others more than they think of themselves? It would make the world so much better."

When we got to Emma's house, we set our backpacks on the bench next to the front door and went into the kitchen.

Her brother Thomas was already in there, making a peanut butter and banana sandwich.

"Thomas, this is Carmen," Emma said as she went to the fridge.

"Hey," Thomas said.

"Hi," Carmen said quietly.

"You want to make us sandwiches, too?" Emma asked her brother.

"You want to wash my underwear?" he responded before he took a big bite of his PB&B.

Emma gave him a friendly slug in the arm as he left the kitchen. "So, what sounds good?" she asked us.

"Not your brother's underwear," I joked.

Emma grimaced. "Definitely not."

She gave us some options and we ended up choosing cheese and crackers along with some apple slices. I helped cut up the apples while Emma sliced some cheese and Carmen put four different kinds of crackers on a plate.

"How does your mom feed so many people?" Carmen asked.

I smiled. "That's what I wondered when I first met them."

"My mom is the queen of menu planning and shopping lists," Emma replied. "And then we all pitch in to help make meals. It's not so bad."

"I whine and complain when I have to make dinner for me and my brother," Carmen said. "And it's only two of us."

"Do you have to do it very often?" Emma asked. "Does your mom work late a lot or something?"

I was glad Emma wasn't afraid to ask her curious questions. All we really knew about Carmen's family was that her brother went to after-school care until five thirty most days, and Carmen was responsible for picking him up and walking him home.

"I don't know," Carmen replied as she slowly and methodically closed up one of the cracker boxes. "It depends. Hey, Emma, can I fill up some glasses with water for us to drink?"

And she'd done it again. Changed the subject.

"Sure," Emma said. She pointed to a corner cupboard. "The glasses are there. Do you guys want to eat at the table or in my room?"

"Your room sounds good," Carmen said. "I want to see it."

Emma checked the clock on the microwave. "Okay. But we don't have a ton of time. I don't want you to be late picking up your brother."

"It's fine, I don't have to walk," Carmen replied. "My mom gave me money to take the bus. So, don't worry."

But I was worried. I was worried Carmen was hiding something from us. And I would have been lying if I'd said I wasn't dying to find out what, exactly, she didn't want us to know about.

Reasons why a person keeps a secret

* *She's afraid of what people might think.*
* *She's afraid of what people might say.*
* *She's afraid of letting someone down.*
* *She's afraid of hurting someone.*
* *She feels ashamed about something.*
* *It feels safer to keep it than to share it, even if that probably isn't true.*
* *She's hiding a gift.*
* *She wants to keep something wonderful and special all to herself.*

(I'm thinking the last two reasons may be the only good reasons to keep a secret.)

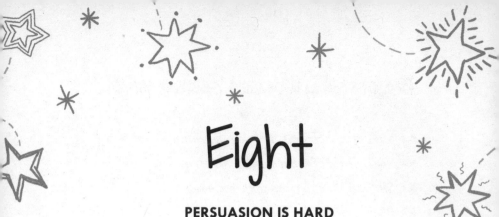

Eight

PERSUASION IS HARD

When we walked into the grocery store, we kind of looked around like little lost children. Where should we go? Who should we ask? It felt like someone had me by the ankles and was swinging me side to side. I was kind of nauseous and dizzy. How were we going to get through this?

Emma turned and looked at us. It was a look that said, "We can do this."

"Come on," Emma said. She sounded very serious and very determined. She walked up to the first checker she saw. "Hello, can you please tell us where we can find the store manager?"

"I'm not sure where he is at the moment." She turned and pointed to a door near the bakery that said AUTHORIZED PERSONNEL ONLY. "The office is through those doors. Go in there and his administrative assistant can help you find him."

"Thank you very much," Emma said.

We followed Emma through the door and up to the

desk that sat a little ways in. A woman with short brown hair, big brown eyes, and a friendly face sat there, working on a computer. "Hello," Emma said. "What's the store manager's name?"

"His name is Mr. Strickland," the woman said.

"Could we speak to him, please?" Emma asked.

"May I ask what this is regarding?" she asked.

"Well," Emma said, "it's kind of hard to explain. Can we just talk to him? Please?"

The woman seemed to think about it for a second before she said, "All right. Let me see if he's available."

We all watched as she walked toward a closed door at the back of the small room.

"You're doing so well," Carmen whispered to Emma.

"Yes," I agreed. "You're amazing, Emma."

She raised her eyebrows. "You guys, we haven't even gotten to the hard part yet."

It was a minute before a tall man with a mustache, wearing a crisp white dress shirt, came out. He wasn't young and he wasn't old. Somewhere in between. In a gruff voice, he said, "Girls, what do you need?"

Both Carmen and I turned and stared at Emma. Her mouth was open slightly, like she was about to speak. But nothing came out.

"Come on," he said as he came closer. "I've got work to do. What is it?"

"Emma?" I finally said.

Still she didn't speak. Didn't even blink. It was like she was in shock or something. I turned back to Mr. Strickland and told myself I should say something, but I couldn't think of the right words. How was I supposed to begin? What points were we going to make? I realized we should have practiced this in Emma's bedroom. Maybe she'd practiced in her head, but she should have practiced it with us, out loud.

Suddenly Emma muttered, "Sorry," then turned around and flew out the door. Not knowing what else to do, I turned around and followed her, and Carmen did the same. Emma didn't stop until she was almost to the bookmobile at the far end of the parking lot.

When she turned to face us, she had tears in her eyes. "I'm so sorry. I couldn't . . . I couldn't do it. He looked so mean and I just . . . I froze."

"It's okay," Carmen said, pulling Emma into a hug.

I rubbed both my friends' backs as I said, "You have nothing to be sorry for."

"Yeah," Carmen said as she pulled away. "We tried. It was harder than we thought it'd be, that's all. We'll do something else."

"But *what*?" Emma said. "I don't know if I can ever walk into that store again."

"How about if we write letters?" Carmen asked. She wiggled her eyebrows. "You two are especially good at that. But this time, instead of putting them into bottles, we'll put them into an envelope and mail them."

"Good idea," I said. "We can do that. Right, Emma?"

"Maybe just the two of you should do it," Emma said. "I might mess things up."

"You know what you need to do?" I asked.

"What?"

I started singing. *"Let it go, let it go . . ."*

Emma and Carmen both burst out laughing. "Oh no, it's contagious," Emma said. "Now I have another thing to be sorry about because breaking out into song is not always a wonderful thing that everyone loves."

"Especially when you're a terrible singer like me," I said.

"You're not terrible," Carmen said. "Trust me. I've heard my dad—"

But she didn't finish. Her hand flew to her mouth as if by mentioning her father, she'd just said a terrible, terrible thing.

"Carmen?" I asked. "It's okay. What about your dad?"

She shook her head. "I'm not supposed to . . . I don't want to talk about him."

Emma and I looked at each other. I saw worry and confusion on her face, and I'm sure she saw the exact same thing on mine.

"Do you have a few more minutes before you have to head home?" Emma asked Carmen. "Because I think we need to have another meeting of the Starry Beach Club."

"Another meeting?" Carmen asked. "But why? We just said we'd go home and write letters. What else is there to discuss?"

Emma put her arm around Carmen. "I think we need to discuss that our club is special and private and that you can trust us. Like, completely."

"We're here for you," I added. "No matter what it is that's going on. And if you need help, we *want* to help you."

She shook her head. "You might change your mind. You *could* change your mind." She shoved her hands into her pants pockets. "I should get going. I don't want to be late. I'll see you guys tomorrow, okay?"

"Carmen," Emma said. "Wait. Are you sure you're all right?"

She didn't answer, though. She only gave us a little nod and a wave as she walked away, down the sidewalk.

I hate that helpless feeling when someone you care about is hurting and there's nothing you can do. And with Carmen, it was even more frustrating because she wouldn't tell us anything. Sometimes my mom says, "You can't help someone who doesn't want to be helped." I'd never quite understood what that meant until now. Unless Carmen opened up to us and let us know what was bothering her, there wasn't much we could do.

"Any idea what's going on?" I asked Emma.

"Nope," she replied. "But can we stop in and see Mr. and Mrs. Button? I could use a little cheering up about now."

"Excellent idea."

When we walked into the bookmobile, Mr. Button was

sitting in his chair reading a book with a moose on the cover while Mrs. Button was back in the shelves.

"Hello, girls," she called out.

"Hi!" we said at the same time.

"It's so nice to see you, Emma and Juliet," Mr. Button said as he set the book down and took off his reading glasses. "Have you come to scour the shelves for a story to transport you to somewhere magical and far away?"

Emma smiled and said, "We mostly came to see you."

"Well, I'm honored to hear that," Mr. Button said. "We always enjoy visiting with you. Anything exciting to share about your weekend? I'd ask you about school, but I don't suppose you really want to talk about that very much."

"I made a banana cream pie," Emma said, "and it was *so* good. There was barely a crumb left after I served it for dessert Saturday night."

"Pie is one of the best things in the world, isn't it?" Mrs. Button said as she came up to see us. "Maybe I should make one myself this week."

"I second the motion!" Mr. Button said. "Especially if it's cherry. Or blackberry. Or coconut cream. Or . . ."

We all laughed. Then Mrs. Button said, "I suppose I will have to make one. But just one. I'm not sure what we would do with three or four pies lying around."

"You could have a pie party," Emma said. "Wouldn't that be fun? Maybe I'll do that someday. Bake a bunch of pies and have a pie party."

I stuck my finger in the air. "Or you could ask everyone to *bring* a pie so you don't have to do all the baking yourself."

"Oooh, I like that idea," Emma said.

"Well, now that we're all hungry for pie, it's about time to close up for the day," Mrs. Button said. "Are you sure you don't want to look for a book, girls?"

"Actually," I said, "do you have any books that teach you how to be convincing?"

"I think we have a book titled *Persuasion*," Mrs. Button said, turning around. "Not the one by Jane Austen, however. It's a nonfiction title. Let me see if I can find it."

"Good idea," Emma whispered.

I had to write a persuasive essay in school once. I wrote about the many reasons dogs should *always* be on leashes when they're not in a fenced yard or in their home. I got an A on it, but we weren't talking about a silly grade now. We were talking about something that would actually make a difference to a whole bunch of people. To me. To Emma. To the Buttons. To the neighborhood.

As we walked through the cozy bookmobile that Mr. and Mrs. Button had made their life's work in their retirement when they could have been doing a hundred different things, I felt like crying. How could anyone think this amazing place filled with books wasn't worth a few parking spots in a parking lot that was never full anyway?

We had to convince Mr. Strickland through our letters to let the bookmobile stay. We just had to.

Dear Mr. Strickland,

I recently moved to San Diego and one of the things I was most excited about was the bookmobile. My grandma told me it was really cute and I would love it, and she was exactly right about that.

Some people might say—but can't you just go to the regular library or your school library? And maybe I can, sometimes. The regular library isn't as easy to get to and the school library is only open during school hours. What if I want a book on Saturday? Or during summer vacation? The bookmobile is there for me, and Mr. and Mrs. Button, two of the sweetest people I've ever met, are there for me. And not just me, lots of other people, too, especially tourists.

I asked Mrs. Button yesterday how many people visited the bookmobile every week, and do you know what she said? On average, they get 225 visitors every week. They're open six days a week, so that's an average of 37.5 people a day. Maybe the .5 is a baby who can't check out by herself, but she still needs books, right?

And what if most of those 37.5 people each day also stop in at your store to pick up some bread or milk or some of your delicious fudge cookies? Do you really want to lose over 200 customers each week who might go to a different store because it's closer to the regular library?

Please let the beach bookmobile stay parked in your lot. Tourists love it. Kids love it. The community loves it. There are so many people who will be upset if it has to close. And if people hear it had to close because of you, they'll be upset with you. And if they're upset with you, they probably won't shop at your store anymore.

Please do the right thing and let the bookmobile stay for free.

Thank you for your time and consideration.

Sincerely,

Juliet Kelley

Nine

CAT'S OUT OF THE BAG

The next day, when Emma and I got off the bus, we split up and went to our lockers, like always. Since I'd arrived as a new student midyear, I'd gotten stuck with one of the lockers at the far end of the red hall. There are three halls in our school and they each have a color assigned—red, blue, and green. Blue hall is in the middle one, and that's where everyone wants to have a locker. That's where Emma has hers. She shares with her friend Shelby. I share with a girl named Apple. Yes, Apple. Like the fruit. Apparently some celebrities I've never heard of named their daughter Apple and my locker partner's parents loved the idea.

"It's so unconventional, right?" she'd said to me when I told her I'd never heard that name. I'm not joking, she actually said that.

"Do you mean something different?" I'd asked.

61

"No," she said with a hint of disgust. "Don't you know anything? Unconventional means unique and cool."

I wanted to ask her if she had a brother named Cucumber (as in cool as a cucumber), but I managed to keep my not-very-nice thoughts to myself.

After I grabbed the books I needed for language arts, I headed to blue hall to find Emma and Carmen. I started to walk over to say hi to Carmen, but she seemed to be in a deep conversation with a couple of people, Mateo and Luciana, and I didn't want to interrupt her.

I wriggled through the sea of people to Emma's locker.

"How's Apple today?" Emma asked.

"Rotten to her core?" I snipped back. She pinched her lips together, trying not to laugh. "I know, I know, I'm a terrible person. I shouldn't say things like that. Forgive me?"

"Of course I forgive you. It's not like we are built to love everyone we meet, right? Some we click with, some we don't. You and Apple don't click, that's all."

"That's for sure," I said. "Any way you slice it." Now I laughed. "Are you tired of my apple puns yet?"

"Never! Funny puns forever and ever."

"This is why we click," I told her.

After Emma grabbed what she needed, we made our way slowly toward Carmen. We wanted to get our letters together, put them in the envelope Emma had brought, and take it to the office to mail. But when we got closer, both of us stopped and stared. Carmen was crying.

"Oh no," I said.

"Um . . . what do we do?" Emma asked.

We watched as Luciana pulled Carmen into a hug. And then both Emma and I turned around and started walking the other way. To do anything else felt wrong, like we were spying on her or invading her privacy or something. Whatever had happened, she'd chosen to tell someone else about it.

When we first met Carmen, she'd mentioned that her best friend, Jovina, had moved away last year. That was one of the reasons she'd wanted to form the Starry Beach Club—to keep her mind off how much she missed her. It was a good plan, too, because I know for me, keeping busy looking for people with wishes had definitely helped me from missing Inca and my old school.

Carmen had told us later that she and Jovina had a bigger group of friends they were a part of, but once Jovina moved away, they'd sort of made Carmen feel like an outsider.

"Is that who Carmen hung around with before?" I asked.

"Yes," Emma said.

"So she's telling them what's bothering her, but not us?"

"She's known them a lot longer," Emma said, trying to make me feel better. "We should be glad she has friends to share things with. Right?"

Of course Emma was exactly right. I didn't want to feel jealous. But emotions aren't something you can choose, like which outfit to wear. They just show up and demand to be noticed. And you can try to tell them to go away, but they aren't always good about listening.

"Maybe she's going to tell us, too," I said, wanting to believe it. "I mean, we haven't seen her yet today. Maybe she saw them first and that's why she told them. It could be something simple like that. Right?"

Emma shrugged. "Right." Then she started singing, *"Don't worry. Be happy."*

We walked by Carmen and her friends and she didn't notice. I'd just have to wait and see if she said anything to us at lunch.

As soon as we finished eating, we asked the monitor for some passes and went to the library. We went to our normal table and before we'd even sat down, Carmen said, "I need to tell you guys something."

"You can tell us anything," Emma said in her kind voice. "We're here for you. Always."

Carmen spoke quickly. "I didn't have time to write my letter. I'm sorry. Last night was super busy. There was a lot going on."

Emma and I looked at each other. "Oh," I said. "That's okay. Two letters is probably enough. Or you could write a short one now, maybe? Only if you want to, though."

"Is everything all right, Carmen?" Emma asked. "We're trying really hard not to worry, but we saw that you were upset this morning. Before school."

"We weren't spying on you or anything like that," I said. "We just noticed as we were walking by. Is there anything we can do?"

Carmen shook her head and picked at her fingernails. "No. There's nothing you can do. There's really nothing anyone can do."

I glanced at Emma and wondered if she would use those superpowers she seems to have in getting people to share their secrets. She'd managed to get me to tell my whole story about my dad and mom splitting up just a couple of hours after meeting her.

"But don't you want to tell us, in case we have an idea for how to help?" Emma said. "Remember, we've already proven we're clever, creative, and diligent. That's why we're part of the Starry Beach Club with you, right?"

"It's just . . ." Carmen's voice trailed off.

"What?" I asked, rubbing her arm. "What is it?"

"I don't want you to think bad things about me."

"We won't," Emma said. "Carmen, you're our friend. And we want to know you better. We really do. That's how friends become close, right? By sharing stuff?"

"The good and the bad," I added.

"It's hard," she said softly, "to tell you. To tell anyone, really. You don't understand what it's like. How scary it is."

I swallowed hard because this seemed to be something much more serious than I'd thought. "But we want to understand. And if you don't tell us what's going on, we never will, you know?"

She leaned in and whispered, "If I tell you, you have to promise not to talk about it outside of your families. Promise?"

"We promise," Emma and I said at the same time.

Carmen nodded as she wrung her hands together. After what seemed like a long time, she took a deep breath before she started speaking quickly but quietly. "I was born in the United States, which means I'm an American citizen. But my parents, they're not. Citizens, I mean. And when I was seven, my father was deported back to Guatemala. Do you know what it means when someone is deported?"

Emma nodded, but I shook my head, because even though I'd heard the word, I didn't know exactly what it meant.

Carmen explained. "The government made him leave this country even though he didn't want to go. He didn't want to leave his family. And he can't come back, no matter how badly he wants to. Like, even if something happened to me or Oscar or my mother, and he wanted to come and see us, he can't. He's not allowed back."

Tears filled her eyes. I reached over and squeezed her hand. She kept talking. "The last day I saw him was at a train station. No one told me where he was going. I didn't really understand why I was saying goodbye.

"For a long time, when people asked about him, I said he was working. He'd call sometimes and my mom would cry and cry after she hung up the phone. I'm not sure how old I was when I figured out he probably wasn't coming back. And when I asked my mom to explain why, she told me that they had both come to this country for a better life. But they weren't citizens, which meant they were here without papers. When she explained everything to me, I was like, you mean you're breaking the law by being here? I didn't understand, you know? In some ways, I still don't. How can trying to live a good life be bad? How can trying to give your kids a good life be a crime? And now . . ."

She stopped talking.

"And now, what?" Emma asked. "Is your mom okay?"

Carmen looked around before she leaned in and whispered again, "They're coming after people like my mom. Even though she's a single mom raising two kids, she's really scared they're going to send her back to Guatemala, too."

"They can't do that, can they?" I asked.

Carmen nodded. "They can. And she's so scared. People we know are always telling us to be careful. Last night, my mom's friend who we live with, Antonia, got pulled over by a police officer because she wasn't wearing a seat belt. Now she'll have to go to court and she's scared that when they learn she's not a citizen, they'll deport her. That's why I didn't write the letter last night. My mom and Antonia were up late talking. They're trying to get her a good lawyer or something. It's just . . ." She paused. "It's so scary. I thought this Starry Beach Club would help keep my mind off the bad stuff, and it does, but it's always there, you know? I can't get rid of the worry, no matter how hard I try."

While Carmen put her head in her hands, Emma rubbed her back. I thought about what my homeroom teacher, Ms. Holland, had said at the beginning of the school year back in Bakersfield. She'd told us that now, more than ever, it was important to be kind and compassionate to everyone. That the principal and the teachers were committed to working hard every day to make our school a safe place for everyone, no matter their race or religion or personal beliefs, and we should each do the same. But outside of school? How could we make the whole world safe? I had no idea.

"Carmen, do you ever get to talk to your dad?" I asked.

She nodded. "We talk to him once a month. And we send him letters and some of our schoolwork to see, and he writes letters to us. I miss him so much. And my poor mom . . ." She sniffled. "She misses him, too. I feel so bad for her. She doesn't know what to do. All she wants is for Oscar and me to be safe. To get a good education. That's why she stays."

"If you ever need a place to go," Emma told her, "you can come to my house. All of you. Anytime. I mean it. Even if it's two o'clock in the morning. My family will do anything we can to help you, I promise."

"Mine, too," I said, although for a second, I wondered what my mom and sister would have to say. They'd want to help, wouldn't they? I decided there was only one way to find out.

Things I've learned about immigration from the internet

* *An immigrant is someone who chooses to move from their country to another one and hopes to live there permanently.*
* *There are lots of reasons people immigrate—to escape war or famine, because they're frightened something might happen to them because of their beliefs, or to just make a better life for themselves.*
* *Almost everyone who lives in the United States comes from a family of immigrants.*
* *The biggest wave of immigration to the United States happened from the 1880s to 1920.*
* *The process to become an American citizen seems complicated.*

(That isn't very much. I want to learn more.)

Ten

NOT FAIR

After school, I went to the bookmobile instead of going straight home. Emma needed to help out at the ice cream shop for a little while, so I went on my own. Mrs. Button was there by herself, sitting at her desk, writing in her notebook of beautiful things.

"Good afternoon, Juliet," she said, looking up at me from behind her reading glasses. "It's so nice to see you."

"Hi, Mrs. Button." I leaned against the little counter. "Can you share something beautiful with me today? I could really use it."

"Aw, I'm sorry you've had a hard day. Here is something I wrote earlier, after a tourist brought their emotional support kitty in here with them." She cleared her throat and read, "Animals have the ability to love unconditionally. It doesn't matter to them what someone looks like or if they're rich or poor or if they have health issues. All that matters is being loved and loving back in return."

"That is so true," I said. "Animals are the best. A lot better than humans, sometimes."

"I think you may be right," she said. "Although that doesn't mean we can't try really hard to be like them, right?"

I smiled. "Right." I paused. "But, Mrs. Button, I feel like I should say, you and Mr. Button don't just try. You do it. You love books and you *really* love sharing books with people. I'm dying to know. Why did you decide to turn a motor home into a bookmobile?"

She smiled. "You probably know that years ago, bookmobiles were a part of the library system. People drove them around and delivered books to rural communities. A mobile library, you see, for people who didn't have a library nearby. Why, the earliest bookmobile was a book wagon, pulled by a horse."

"Wow. Really?"

"Yes," she said. "The bookmobile has quite an interesting history. My mother used to tell me stories of visiting the bookmobile as a child when it came to her little town in Mississippi. She said the black children were especially excited because they weren't allowed to go into the regular library."

It made my heart hurt, thinking about people not being able to get books just because of the color of their skin. "That's so wrong," I said. "I don't understand why some people are so hateful."

"I know. Me either. My mother grew up to be a successful attorney, fighting for civil rights. She was my hero. Anyway, I always thought it sounded like such a wonderful thing to do—delivering books to people who needed them. Not many people know this, but for a while after I retired from my librarian job, Mr. Button and I drove this bookmobile around small towns in Eastern Oregon. My parents had gifted us with a cabin they'd owned when they were alive, and we lived there for a time. Juliet, Eastern Oregon is one of the most beautiful places I've ever seen. But as we got older, we decided we'd like to settle in one place. A sunny place, by the beach. And so, we ended up here. We took most of our inheritance money from my folks and transformed the bookmobile into what it is today."

I thought of the boy painted on the front, reading a book in front of a giant sand castle. "Bookmobile by the beach," I said.

"I know sometimes people think it's silly, having a bookmobile when there's a perfectly good library not too far. But we figure we're not hurting anyone. And the tourists sure seem to appreciate us."

"Lots of people appreciate you," I said. "Including me!"

Mrs. Button stood up and gave me a smile that made me feel the way I did while eating a warm muffin, fresh out of the oven. "Well, thank you. You're very sweet to say that. I do believe it's important for retirees to find things that give them purpose, and this bookmobile has done that for us. We'll have to wait and see what new adventures await us, I suppose."

I knew she was thinking about what might happen if they couldn't stay in the store parking lot. If Mr. Strickland kicked them off the property because they didn't have extra money to pay rent. It almost made me tear up, thinking about it.

"So tell me, Juliet, how can I help you today? Do you need help finding something or do you want to look around?"

"I was wondering if you had any books about immigrants? Or immigration? Nothing too boring, though."

She chuckled as she walked over to the stacks and looked around before turning back to me. "No. I'd never want to give you something boring. Although I'm sad to say our little library doesn't have anything for you. The city library, with lots more books than we have here, is probably better suited for your request." She scanned the shelves as if she was checking to make sure. "I'm sorry, Juliet. I feel terrible that I can't help you."

"It's okay. I figured it was worth a try. Thank you."

"Thanks for stopping in," she said.

"See you later," I told her as I headed back outside.

"Bye," she said.

Outside, the smell of chocolate made my stomach growl.

The bakery was probably making those fudge cookies I loved so much. It took all my willpower not to march in there and buy one for a snack. I'd promised myself that I wouldn't shop there until the manager changed his mind and let the bookmobile stay.

And what a coincidence that at the very moment when I thought about him, I glanced at the store before heading for home and saw Mr. Strickland in the parking lot. He was talking to an older woman wearing purple glasses and a skirt with colorful pictures of doughnuts. Who was it? A customer? An employee? I couldn't quite tell. But then the woman reached up and gave him a hug, and it seemed like neither one of those guesses was probably correct. She was too old to be his wife, wasn't she? Maybe it was an aunt or even his mother. Or maybe it was a very kind person hugging him before telling him he was fired for being the worst store manager in the history of the world. Well, a person can dream, can't they?

I snapped a photo and sent it to Emma with a text:

Can you believe he's hugging someone? That means he actually has a heart. Probably a tiny black one, though. Who do you think it is? That he's hugging?

Emma texted back a minute later.

My mom says it's his mother. She knows her. Says she's very nice. Is that even possible? For nice mothers to have mean children?

I was pretty sure it was *very* possible, which made me

wish, once again, that the world made more sense than it did.

That night, the three of us were all home for dinner. Miranda and I made tacos, the delicious smell of spices and onion filling up the house.

When Mom got home from work, she said, "Thanks, girls," as she threw her briefcase on the sofa and eyed the table we'd set along with the bowls filled with shredded cheese, chopped lettuce, and diced tomatoes. "Such a big help. Do I have time to change or not?"

"We should probably eat now unless you like cold tacos," Miranda said.

Mom took a seat and put a napkin in her lap. "Now works for me."

Miranda talked about a project she was working on for school, so I ate quickly, wanting to be done so I could ask Mom the question that had been on my mind since lunch.

"What about you, Juju Bean?" Mom asked. "Anything exciting happening with you?"

"I want to ask you something," I told her.

"Okay. Go for it."

"If someone felt afraid . . ." I stopped, trying to think how to word it exactly. "If a family who was here from another country felt afraid that they were going to be caught and the mom might be sent back to the country she came from, what would you say to them?"

Mom stared at me for a moment as she wiped her mouth. "Hm. Well, now. That's quite the question. I think I'd probably tell them a good immigration lawyer might be helpful."

"Is that all?" I asked.

"I'm not sure what you're getting at, Juliet. Is this someone you know?"

"Yes."

"Someone from school?"

"Yes. My friend Carmen. And Emma told Carmen that they were welcome at their house anytime, if they needed a place to stay. And I guess I'm wondering if you feel the same."

Mom pushed her plate forward, then folded her hands as she rested her elbows on the table. "Of course they're welcome here, sweetie. I would never turn away someone who needed help. How did this come up, anyway?"

I told Mom and Miranda everything Carmen had told us, hoping Carmen wouldn't mind. She had made us promise not to tell anyone outside of our families, which meant she understood it's hard to keep things from your parents. And I trusted my family. It wasn't like they were going to turn them in or something terrible like that.

"The immigration issue is a complex one," Mom said. "There are no easy answers. But Carmen was born here?"

"Yes. Her younger brother, too."

"Well," Mom said, "like I said earlier, hopefully they're working with a lawyer who will help Carmen's mom become a citizen."

"What would happen to her kids if she was deported?" I asked.

Mom bit her lip before she finally said, "Unfortunately, they'd probably be put into foster care."

Miranda stood up and gathered our dinner plates. "It's so sad that they have to live in fear of their mom being sent away. That does not sound like a fun way to live. At all."

"No," Mom replied. "Not to mention they probably miss Carmen's father terribly."

I couldn't help but think of my dad. How I'd been disappointed about our weekend together and, afterward, how I wasn't too excited about going back. Carmen wouldn't have cared if she'd had to sleep on the floor of her dad's place. She wouldn't have cared if the weekend was about as exciting as watching a golf match. All that would have mattered was being with her dad. Maybe that's why she'd been so curious about my weekend in Bakersfield—maybe there was a little bit of jealousy underneath the questions she asked me.

It made me feel bad that I had complained at all about the weekend. Carmen would probably give anything to see her dad again.

Life is just not fair.

Things I wish I could give Carmen

* *A smile*
* *A visit with her dad*
* *A good book that will help her to forget her troubles*
* *Her favorite painting by Vincent van Gogh,*
  Seascape near Les Saintes-Maries-de-la-Mer
* *Citizenship for her mom*

Eleven

THE INVISIBLE SHARK

That night, after I did my homework, I decided since I couldn't give Carmen a painting by her favorite artist, I'd give her one painted by me. It wouldn't solve any of her problems, but maybe it would cheer her up. I could only hope.

The thing I love about painting is that once I start and get swept up in the creation and the colors, it's a little like getting lost in a good story. The world kind of fades away and it's just me and the canvas and nothing else matters for a while.

I decided to paint her a picture of the beach. I painted the ocean and the sand and then, on the sand, I painted a little dark-haired boy kneeling next to a tall sand castle. I'm not very good at drawing people, but I painted him so he was facing away so I didn't have to worry about getting his face right, only the back of his head. I also created the scene so it was like someone looking down at the beach from a high cliff far away. Hopefully she'd know I meant for the boy to be her brother.

Mom came in just as I was finishing up. "May I take a peek?"

She knew to ask ever since I got upset with her one time for looking without checking with me first. Sometimes I'm not happy with how something turns out and I don't want anyone to see it. Other times I'm thrilled to share what I've done. But it depends, and I want to be the one who decides whether she sees one of my paintings or not.

"Sure," I said. "It's for Carmen."

She walked around and stood in front of my easel. "Oh, Juju Bean, it's wonderful. I love the way you painted the sun setting in the horizon. Is the little boy her brother?"

"Yes," I said. "His name is Oscar. He loves building sand castles. The first time I saw her she was at the beach and that's what they were doing."

"I think she's going to love it," Mom said, pulling me in for a hug. "You're a good friend."

"I wish I could do more," I told her.

"I know you do. But we need to remember that sometimes being a helpful friend doesn't mean *doing* something, it means just being there. Listening. Comforting. And even doing fun things together to get her mind off her problems, yeah?"

I nodded. She was exactly right. I needed to keep us focused on our club and making wishes come true.

On Saturday, we had a Starry Beach Club meeting at the beach. It was a warm, sunny spring day, so we decided to meet for a picnic lunch. Emma brought turkey sandwiches; I brought some bananas, chips, and three dill pickles; and Carmen brought a blackberry Gatorade to share. We spread everything out on a blanket Emma had brought along and sat facing one another.

"Juliet, I hung the painting you gave me in my room," Carmen said. "It looks good. Oscar loves it, too. And that's important since we . . . share." She looked down and brushed sand off the blanket. "Our apartment isn't big enough for me to have my own room. We have a sheet hung up in the middle, though, and he's pretty good about staying on his side. I hung the painting by the door so we both see it when we're going out."

"Did he know it was him in the painting when he saw it?" I asked.

She smiled. "Yeah. He knew right away. He loved that you painted him and not me. Like that made him extra special."

"Did you give the painting a name?" Emma asked as she pulled the sandwiches out of a paper bag. "You have to name it. That's what artists do, right?"

"Um, okay. How about *Don't Get Sand in Your Shorts*?" I thought on it some more. "Or *The Invisible Shark*."

"Wait, what?" Carmen asked. "What shark? I didn't see a shark in the picture."

"Right. That's why I said *The Invisible Shark*."

"Do I need to worry about the invisible shark eating my brother?" she asked.

"You never let him go in the water anyway, right?" I asked. "So he's fine. The invisible shark will leave him alone, I promise."

"Oh, good," Carmen said, and the way she said it, like she had really been afraid of a shark getting her brother in a *painting*, made us laugh.

"I have a better idea," Emma said. "How about *Happy Boy at the Beach*?"

"That's perfect," Carmen said. "And someday you'll be famous, Juliet, and I can sell it for a million dollars. Invisible shark and all."

"Did you sign it?" Emma asked.

"Yes," I said. "I always do. But not because I think my paintings are going to be worth a lot of money someday. My dad asked me to sign the first painting I did for him and then I just kept doing it." Realizing what I'd said, I reached out and gently grabbed Carmen's hand. "Sorry. I'll try not to talk about my dad. I don't want to make you miss yours."

She squeezed my hand before she let go. "Please don't. I feel like that's asking the impossible."

"But if it makes you sad . . ." Emma said.

"It's okay," Carmen said. "Really. I don't want you to feel like you have to be careful around me all the time, worried you might say the wrong thing, you know? Now, can we eat? I'm starving."

As I ate my sandwich, I looked out at the ocean and imagined an invisible shark. Imagined something lurking there, something we couldn't see. If we didn't know about it, we had no reason to be afraid. But that isn't how the world works. If only all sharks were invisible and they kept their distance so everyone stayed safe.

If only Carmen had no reason to be afraid.

Things that are invisible

* *Hope*
* *Magic*
* *Dust mites (ewwww)*
* *Hunger*
* *Thirst*
* *Imagination*
* *Air*
* *Gravity*
* *Love*

Twelve

A NEW PLAN

"So," Emma said. "I have to tell you guys something."

She sounded serious. I picked up a pickle and took a bite. "Okay."

"It's not good," she said with a little shake of her head.

"Uh-oh," Carmen said. "What's happened?"

"Mr. Strickland called my dad last night," Emma said.

It felt like someone had pounced on me from behind. Of all the things she could have said, I was not expecting that. "No way."

"Yep," Emma said. "He told my dad we need to stop pestering him about things that aren't any of our business."

My stomach felt queasy. Was this really happening? "Are you serious?"

"Yep. He actually used the word *pestering*. Can you believe it?"

"What'd your dad say?" I asked, munching on my pickle

so hard, I had to tell myself to be careful or I might miss my target and bite my tongue off.

"He told Mr. Strickland that the three of us felt strongly about the bookmobile and we weren't doing anything wrong by asking him to think about changing his mind. I know because I was sitting right there while he talked to him. He rolled his eyes while he listened to Mr. Strickland go on and on about how hard it is successfully run a grocery store and he's only doing what he has to do to stay in business. I couldn't hear Mr. Strickland, but after they hung up, Dad told me that's what he said."

"I can't believe he called your dad," I said. "Did he think you'd get punished or something?"

"Yeah, he probably hoped I'd get grounded for the rest of my life so he'd never have to see me again. But that's not all he said. Want to know the real reason he wants the bookmobile to leave?"

I froze.

"Why?" Carmen asked.

"He wants to put something else in its spot."

"He does?" I said. "What? What is it?"

"He wants to put a giant hot dog stand there," Emma replied. "He thinks the tourists are absolutely dying for hot dogs."

"Hot dogs?" Carmen said. "Gross."

"I'll admit, I like hot dogs—but I'd pick a book over a

hot dog every time," I said. "Like, it could be the best hot dog in the world and I'd still want a book instead."

"What about pickles?" Emma asked as she picked hers up and munched on it.

"That is the worst which-would-you-rather question ever," I told her. "Please. Don't make me pick one."

Emma smiled. "Okay, we won't. So, what are we going to do now?"

"I don't know," I said. "But my family is never shopping at that store again. I'm so mad, you guys."

Carmen finished her sandwich and wiped her face and hands with a napkin. "There are a lot better stores we can go to anyway. It's so expensive, you know? That's why my mom doesn't shop there."

"He's a greedy, selfish man," I said. "He probably thinks he's going to make millions selling expensive hot dogs to clueless, hungry tourists."

"We should protest," Emma said.

"Protest?" I asked. "You mean, like, march in front of the store carrying signs?"

"Yes!" Emma said. "We could make signs that say something like, 'Books are better for you than hot dogs.'"

"Except no one would understand why we were saying that," Carmen said. "Since no one but us knows that he's thinking about putting a hot dog stand there. It might make us look . . ."

"Like silly kids," I said. "Yeah, she's right. We need to think of something else."

"Can't we try and find a different place for the bookmobile to park?" Carmen asked.

"The thing is, the Buttons like it there," I said. "And it's the perfect spot, really."

"So, we have to find a way to pay the rent," Emma said. "Right? That's the only thing we can do now?"

"Seems like it," I said. "Any ideas?"

"How about squirrel monkeys with donation cups?" Emma joked. "Like in the olden days when men played accordions with monkeys on their shoulders?"

"Oh, the poor monkeys," Carmen said.

"You should go to college and major in animal science and study the monkeys you love so much, Carmen," I said. "You could become like another Jane Goodall. But with squirrel monkeys instead of chimpanzees."

"I'd love that," Carmen said. "My mom works so hard, cleaning houses and working odd jobs, and I don't want my life to be like that. I mean, no disrespect to my mom. I love her and she's doing the best she can, but . . ."

"It's okay," Emma said. "You don't have to explain. We understand."

As we finished our lunch, we tossed around ideas about how we could raise money to help Mr. and Mrs. Button. Some of the usual fund-raising ideas were mentioned: bake sale, car wash, raffle for some fantastic donated prize. But they all seemed overdone and like they'd be a lot of work.

"What about an event where we sold stuff?" Carmen said. "Not baked goods or things people have seen a million times. Good stuff, that people would want to buy. And then part of the money could go to the bookmobile?"

"Like what?" I asked.

"Like . . . your paintings?" Carmen asked.

"Oh my gosh, yes!" Emma said, bouncing up and down on her knees. "That's such a good idea!"

All I could do was sit there and stare at them. I stared like an owl with two big eyes who just kept blinking and blinking as they talked about me and my paintings. They talked as if this was the best idea in the history of the universe. Meanwhile, all I could think about was how it was absolutely the *worst* idea in the history of the universe.

I'm not sure how, exactly, but somehow I found my voice and owl girl became a regular girl again. "No," I said, quietly at first. The second time, it was louder. "No. That is not a good idea at all. You guys, no one will want to buy my paintings. That's banana pants. Seriously."

"It's not banana pants, Juliet," Emma said. "You are so talented."

"I understand why you might be nervous," Carmen said. "What about this? What if we made it so it's not just you, but other people selling things they've made, too?"

"You mean, make it an arts and crafts fair?" Emma

asked. "Usually those are in the winter, though. Around the holidays."

"Is there a rule they can't happen other times of the year?" Carmen asked.

"No," Emma said. "We'd just need to figure out a way to make people excited about an arts and crafts fair in the spring, when they don't have gifts to buy for anyone." Suddenly, her eyes got big and round. "Wait, I know! Mother's Day! We could make it an arts and crafts fair for Mother's Day. *Bring your mom and shop.* Or *Come and shop for your mom.* Something like that? That could work, right?"

I had to admit, it sounded like a really good idea, but every time I even thought about putting my artwork in a booth for people to see—and judge, because they would—it felt like I was about to break into hives. Plus, Mother's Day wasn't that far away. If I somehow managed to find enough courage to sell my paintings, would I have enough time to get ready?

"Let's keep brainstorming," I suggested. "I bet we can think of something even better. Besides, where would we have it? We'd probably have to pay to borrow a space somewhere for the day and we need to *raise* money, not spend money."

Emma started putting our picnic stuff back into the bag she'd brought. "Maybe we could get someone to donate a place. You know who we can ask? Who might have an idea about that? Mr. Dooney. He knows a lot of people."

"Can't we come up with some other ideas first?" I asked. I was begging my brain to think of something brilliant, but nothing came to me. Not a single thing. Oh brain, why do you have to fail me when I need you the most?

Emma turned to me, and her eyes were loving. Kind. "Juliet, I know you're nervous about selling your paintings, but it'll be fine! You can even keep some of the money and buy something special for yourself. Like, I'm thinking we ask people to donate to a fund for the bookmobile based on what they sell. Because people might not want to do it if they think they have to give all the money they make. I don't know, we'll have to think about it. I'll ask my parents about it, too, and see what they say. But I promise, it will be fine. People are going to love your work."

She sounded so sure, but there was absolutely no way for her to know that. I kept imagining what would happen if I put out a bunch of paintings and no one bought them. It'd be so embarrassing. Like, I'd rather burp during a quiet scene in a packed movie theater than not sell a single painting. Or walk around school with pants that had ripped in the rear. Okay, maybe not that, but still. Did they realize what it would feel like for me if I didn't sell anything?

Emma stood up. "Come on. Let's go talk to Mr. Dooney and see if he has any ideas."

"Can I go swim with the invisible sharks instead?" I asked.

"You're funny," Carmen said.

The really funny thing? I wasn't even joking.

Things I can say to try to sell my paintings

* *I'm eleven years old and this is my first art show and I don't want to die of embarrassment at such a young age.*
* *This is a picture of my cat, Casper, and he will love you forever if you buy it for your home.*
* *This painting is only ten dollars. That's less than the cost of most pizzas and it lasts a lot longer.*
* *I painted this cute narwhal for someone just like you. That is, someone who smiles just thinking about a creature called "the unicorn of the sea."*
* *Make an offer. I'll take anything over fifty cents.*
* *You can have five for the price of one. They make wonderful gifts. You can even give them to people you don't like very much if you want to.*
* *Don't make me beg. Please.*

Thirteen

I WISH IT WAS EASIER

"Well, look who's here," Mr. Dooney said when we walked up to his house. He was sitting on his patio that faced the boardwalk, in the same spot where I'd first met him. He got up and came over to meet us. "What can I do for you, girls?"

"First of all, Mr. Dooney, this is our friend Carmen," I said. "Carmen, this is Mr. Dooney."

"Nice to meet you," Mr. Dooney said.

"Thanks. You, too," Carmen said.

"We've come to ask you a favor," Emma said.

"Well, isn't that wonderful," Mr. Dooney said as he took his striped cap off and rubbed his practically bald head. "I'm happy to assist if I'm able after you did such a nice thing for me."

Carmen spoke next. "We're trying to find a way to help Mr. and Mrs. Button. Help them keep the bookmobile in their spot at the grocery store, you know? The new manager

93

is going to make them pay rent. So we were thinking we'd organize a Mother's Day arts and crafts fair. But we don't know where we could have it."

"Yeah," Emma chimed in. "We were wondering if maybe you know someone who might let us have it in a big space for free?"

He gave his head another rub before he put his hat back on. "Oh, boy. That's a tough one. Let me think on it, okay? And I can maybe do some asking around, how does that sound?"

"That sounds really good," Emma said.

"I can't make any promises, of course," Mr. Dooney said. "Though I assure you, I'll do my very best."

"Thank you so much," Emma said.

"Yeah. Thank you," Carmen said.

They both looked at me and I knew I needed to say something. "If you don't find anything, it's totally okay. We can come up with something else."

"Juliet," Emma said with a little laugh. "It's gonna happen. And you'll be fine." She started singing, *"Don't stop believing."*

"Are you worried about something?" Mr. Dooney asked me.

Before I had a chance to answer, Emma answered for me. "We told her she should sell some of her beautiful paintings, but she's afraid no one will want to buy them."

"I understand," Mr. Dooney said in a soft voice. "Putting yourself out there for the world to see is not easy. Believe me, I know."

"You do?" Carmen asked. "Are you an artist?"

"Oh, no. I couldn't draw a picture if my life depended on it. No, I was an author once upon a time."

"You wrote books?" I asked him.

"I sure did," he said. "Western novels. Back in the good old days when people loved reading about the Wild West."

"Wow," Emma said. "That's amazing, Mr. Dooney."

"Writing a novel is a lot of work, but also a lot of fun," he replied. "And of course, I understand your love of books and wanting to keep the bookmobile where it is. I feel the same. So let's see what we can do, okay?"

"Okay!" Emma and Carmen said.

I just smiled. Sort of.

As we walked to Emma's house a little while later to hang out, I thought about the time when Dad asked me to sign my name on my painting. I'm not sure how old I was. Four, I think? I'd painted an apple tree. It was one of those big, bushy trees kids draw because they're easy. First you draw a trunk and then you basically draw a green cloud on top of the trunk. But I hadn't stopped there. I'd added red dots. Apples. My dad made me feel like it was the best painting he'd ever seen.

"It's spectacular," he'd told me. I specifically remember

that's what he said. But it wasn't about the words, it was about the way it made me feel. Like I was truly an artist who had created something beautiful.

And then he told me all great artists signed their work, usually in the corner. So I'd written my first name as small as I could (which wasn't very small at all) in the right-hand corner and Dad had told me something like, "I hope you'll paint a lot more pictures in the coming years, Juliet. But I'm keeping this one forever, because it's your first original piece."

Maybe his reaction was the reason I still loved painting trees. I don't know. All I know is back then, sharing my art with him had been so easy. And maybe deep down I knew he'd love it no matter what, because that's what parents do. They love you and they love the work you do. But now, sharing art even with my mom wasn't exactly easy. I only wanted her to see the pieces that I thought were my best.

In school, during art literacy class, when we studied Vincent van Gogh's painting *The Starry Night*, our teacher told us that Vincent's brother was his biggest supporter. Letters between the brothers showed how much Theo had loved and supported him, which often carried him through hard times. She told us that while it's wonderful to have someone who loves your work, it's important that you love the process of creating and enjoy bringing something new into the world more than you love other people's approval.

I've thought about that a lot. But it's so hard to *not* want people's approval. It feels so good to have someone say they love something I've made, the way Carmen did when I gave her *Happy Boy at the Beach*. And if you're going to give your art away, or sell it, don't you need other people to like it?

It's all very confusing to me. All I know is I love painting. I love making something from nothing. But thinking about someone maybe walking into a booth, looking around, and walking away while whispering to her mom, "Those were the ugliest paintings I've ever seen" made my stomach hurt. How do you make yourself not care about that?

When we got to Emma's house, Joanne was sitting in the family room, reading a book. "Hello, girls, so nice to see you. How was the picnic?"

"It was good, thanks," Emma said. "We're going to hang out in my room for a while, is that okay? It was getting kind of windy on the beach."

"That's perfectly fine," her mom said. "I'm going to go to the shop here in a few minutes. Your dad offered to give me some time to myself, so I happily took it. But I know he has things he needs to do. I think Molly's in her room, so you won't be here alone."

"We'll be fine," Emma said.

Joanne smiled. "Yes, I know. But sometimes it's just nice to know someone's here, right?"

"With a big family, someone's probably always around, right?" Carmen asked.

"Pretty much," Emma said as she headed for the stairs. "It can be kind of annoying, actually."

"I would love it," Carmen said softly. "I would love it so much."

And just like that, it seemed ridiculous that I was worrying about my feelings when it came to my artwork when Carmen had much bigger things to worry about.

How I feel when I'm painting

* *I'm so excited—I'm going to paint something!*
* *This is going to be my best one yet!*
* *Okay, maybe not the best one. But good. Hopefully.*
* *Is this even good?*
* *It's okay, I can still fix it. Maybe.*
* *Hm. Do I even like it?*
* *A little more work will make it better.*
* *Keep working. Keep trying. It's getting there.*
* *I wish it was my best. Maybe next time.*
* *I like it, though. But will anyone else?*

Fourteen

NOTHING MAKES SENSE

When I got home, I really, really wanted to talk to Inca. But it'd been almost a week since our disastrous doughnut date and she hadn't texted me once. It didn't seem fair. Why did I have to be the one to try to end this weird thing between us? But I needed someone to listen and understand what I was feeling, instead of telling me I was wrong to feel nervous about showing my art. And I knew I could count on Inca to listen.

Mom and Miranda were both out. They'd texted me to let me know they were doing some shopping. It was the perfect time to reach out to Inca if I was going to do it. I told myself there was no reason to be anxious. She and I had been friends for a long time. She was the kind of friend who let me cry in her room after I learned my parents were separating. That kind of friendship doesn't just disappear in a matter of a few weeks, does it? I decided it wouldn't as long as I didn't let it.

I sat at the computer and opened Skype and clicked on

Inca's name. I was amazed when she answered and her face popped up on my screen.

"Hey!" I said.

"Hi."

"What are you doing?" I asked.

She tucked her hair behind her ears. "Waiting to go to the movies with Ariel."

"Oh. Fun. I, um . . ."

And just like that, I couldn't think of a thing to say. It felt like last Sunday all over again. This wasn't how it was supposed to go. She was supposed to be happy to see me and maybe tell me she was sorry she hadn't texted me to make sure everything was all right.

"Is everything okay?" she asked.

I wondered if I looked like I was about to cry. I felt like I was about to cry.

"I just, I miss you, that's all," I said. "Things feel . . . different."

"I know," she said. There was kindness in her voice and it made me so happy to hear it. "Things *are* different. I miss you, too."

"You do?" I asked as I blinked back tears.

"Well, yeah. Why wouldn't I, silly? Do you know how awful P.E. is without you?"

"Is Maverick still being his totally obnoxious self?"

"What do you think? Some things change, but a lot of things stay the same, too."

Hearing her say this made me feel so much better. I mean, not the stuff about Maverick. Mean people are awful and all of that. But this was the friend I knew and loved. The friend who cared and seemed to say just the right thing when I needed it. I wanted to tell her everything that was happening. I wanted to tell her about my disappointing weekend at Dad's. About the situation with Emma and Carmen. About how scared Carmen was for her mom and how I was scared for her. "My new friends—"

But I didn't get to finish, because just then, Inca's door opened and her mom said, "Ariel and her mom are here."

"Sorry, I gotta go," she told me. "But it was good to talk to you."

"Oh. Yeah. You, too."

She waved and smiled. "Bye!"

"Bye."

As I turned off the computer, it felt like being at a restaurant and having the waiter walk by with a piece of chocolate and peanut butter pie, the best kind of pie in the world, but when you order it, he says, "Sorry, we're all out." All I wanted was to have a good heart-to-heart with my best friend and just when I thought it might happen, she had to go. *So* not fair.

I tried to tell myself that at least I knew things were okay between us. She missed me and I missed her and hopefully we'd find some time to talk again soon. It made me feel bad that I had left so suddenly last weekend. I probably should have given it more of a chance to work itself out.

I stood up, and when I did, my two paintings on the shelf on the wall caught my eye. One was a tree, the other was an owl. I thought back to when Emma had stopped by one day and said how much she loved them. She had told me she'd happily pay me to paint her something, but I'd told her I'd do one for free, and I had. I'd painted her a picture of Casper, on a black canvas, because when she'd met him, she'd told me that she'd always wanted a white kitty. Since she couldn't have one because some of her family members were allergic, I figured she could have the next best thing—a painting of one. She was thrilled when I gave it to her.

Why was I able to give her one, and Carmen, too, but the thought of painting for strangers scared me so much? It seemed kind of backward. Was it because I felt safe with my friends? That I was sure they would never say something mean?

I wanted it to make sense. More than that, I wanted to be as excited about the arts and crafts fair as my friends were. The Starry Beach Club was all about making wishes come true, and we had a chance to work together to make a wish come true for two of our favorite people. Couldn't I just get over it and do it for them?

Just then, there was a knock at the front door. I went to the window to check before opening it, just like Mom had taught me. When I flung the door open, I said, "Grandma, you're back!"

"Juliet!" she said as she took me in her arms and gave me a long, wonderful hug. She smelled like her favorite lavender-scented lotion. Then she stepped inside and looked around. "Your mom had told me she was hoping to buy some local artwork for the place. Must still be looking, huh?"

"Yeah," I said. "She's just been really busy with the new job. She and Miranda are out shopping right now—maybe they'll bring something home. Is Grandpa parking the car?"

"No, he wasn't feeling well, so he stayed home. I just decided to drive down and see all of you. I still feel awful that we were out of the country when you were moving in." She glanced around the room again and smiled. "Looks like you've managed pretty well on your own, though."

Grandma doesn't look sixty-five at all. She looks more like fifty, with her tall, slim build, her dyed blond hair, and her stylish tortoiseshell eyeglasses. Before she retired last year, she was vice president of a temp agency. I guess she did a really good job, because when she announced her retirement, they begged her to stay. But she told them it was time to do other things, and she seems to be happy with her decision.

"Did you get my postcards?" she asked.

"We got one from Paris, one from London, and one from Dublin."

"Oh, good," she said.

"Thank you for sending them," I said. "Which city was your favorite?"

Grandma walked over to the shelf with my artwork and lovingly traced the owl with her finger. "None of them, actually. My favorite was a place I'd like to take you someday. A charming little town about an hour outside Paris where Vincent van Gogh spent his last remaining days. It's called Auvers-sur-Oise. Have you heard of it?"

"I think I read about it," I said. "In one of the books I checked out about Vincent. Are he and his brother buried there?"

She turned and looked at me. "Yes. In very simple graves at the back of the cemetery. And all over the village are prints of his paintings that he did while he lived there. He painted one just about every day leading up to his death, because his doctor told him it would do him good. He was so talented, wasn't he? It's sad that he didn't see it. Or couldn't see it."

"Do you think most artists are that way?" I ask. "Like, not able to see their talent?"

"I don't really know," she said. "I'm not particularly artistic myself, remember. I think every artist must deal with some insecurities, and part of making art is probably figuring out what works and what doesn't in dealing with those insecurities."

"You know Mr. Dooney, right?" I asked.

She smiled. "Oh, yes. We've been friends for a long time. I sure do miss his wife, Patricia. I know he does, too."

"Today, he told me that he used to be an author. He wrote Western novels."

"Yes, isn't that something? I actually read a few of them. They were quite good, too."

"I want to ask him if he ever felt nervous showing his work to people."

"I'm sure he'd be happy to talk to you about that," Grandma said. "He's a very nice man." She walked toward the kitchen. "Do you think your mom and sister will be back soon?"

"I'll text them and tell them you're here," I said. "That'll get them home fast."

"I'll take you out to dinner later, how's that sound?"

"Sounds good to me, Grandma." And I really meant it. There's just something special, comforting even, about spending time with your grandma.

Things I wish I could ask Vincent van Gogh

* *Which painting of yours is your favorite? I bet we'd be surprised by your answer.*
* *Did you worry a lot about what people would think of your art?*
* *If you did worry, how were you able to keep painting?*
* *Did you ever think about giving up?*
* *What's your number one piece of advice for a young artist like me?*
* *What's your favorite color?*
* *Do you like pickles?*
* *How did you die? Really? I want to know the truth. More and more people think it was actually some kind of accident.*
* *Do you wish you were alive so you could see how much your art means to people? I do.*

Fifteen

CRASHING WAVES

The following Friday, the Starry Beach Club went to Mr. Dooney's house after school together.

"I hope he has an amazing place for us," Emma said, swinging her arms extra hard as we walked. She seemed very . . . excited. "My mom and my sister both said they'd be willing to pitch in and help us organize the event. We'll need to get the word out quickly, so they'll be a big help."

"Are you sure we have enough time?" I asked. "I mean, for the people who want to sell stuff?"

"I think a lot of people who like to do booths have their crafts ready," Emma said. "Like, my mom's friend Susan, who knits blankets and hats? The last time I was at her house, she had a whole tub of items just waiting for the next arts and crafts fair."

That was smart. That way, she wasn't stressing about making a bunch of things in a short amount of time like

108

I would be if everything came together and we went ahead with the fair.

Carmen had been pretty quiet on the bus ride home, but now she spoke up. "I told my mom about it and she'd like to have a booth but she's kind of scared. Not about selling her stuff, just . . . about being in public like that."

"I'm sorry she feels that way," I said. "What does she make?"

"She makes necklaces out of paper," Carmen said. "She uses colorful pages from magazines and folds them so they look like beads. They're really beautiful. I've tried to do it and it's hard. She's so good at it, though."

"Hey!" Emma said. "I know. You can sell them for her. You're a kid. No one will give you a hard time."

"But what if they ask me if I made them?" Carmen asked. "I don't want to lie, you know?"

"Can you help her put a few together?" I asked. "Like string them together or even put price tags on them? That way, you could just say you and your mom made them together and you'd be telling the truth."

"Hm," she replied. "Maybe. Good idea. How many paintings are you going to try and sell?"

"Twenty!" Emma exclaimed. "No. How about fifty? I bet if you took fifty, you'd sell them all."

"I wish I had your confidence," I said.

She rubbed my arm and grinned. "There. I just gave you some. Feel it?"

If only it were that easy.

"If I do this, I want to have paintings that people will love," I said, "and I'm not sure I can do that in such a short amount of time. I only have one or two at my house ready to go."

"They don't have to be complicated, right?" Emma said. "So, keep it simple."

I wasn't sure I knew how to do that. With every painting, I try to give it my all. I want it to be the best it can be. It's not that I was trying to be complicated; I was trying to be a good artist.

When we got to Mr. Dooney's, he wasn't on his patio, since it wasn't exactly patio weather. So we knocked on his door, and when he answered, he invited us into his house.

"You've come at the perfect time," he said. "I have good news. And someone here to tell you that good news. Please, come into the kitchen. We were just having some lemonade. Would you like some? I might even have some vanilla wafers, too, if you're hungry."

Emma looked at us and shrugged. "We're eleven-year-olds. We're always happy to eat. Or that's what my dad says, anyway."

When we walked into the kitchen, I froze when I saw who was there.

"Anne Marie, I'd like you to meet the girls who are organizing the Mother's Day arts and craft fair. This is

Emma, Juliet, and Carmen. Girls, this is Ms. Anne Marie Strickland. She works at the senior center and they have a large space that would be perfect for your event."

"So nice to meet you," Ms. Strickland said.

I couldn't speak. I'm guessing Emma couldn't either, since she was probably as shocked as I was. It was probably good that Carmen didn't seem to know what was going on because she was able to say something for us.

"It's very nice to meet you, too," she said.

"Anne Marie has an application for you to fill out," Mr. Dooney said as he picked up a piece of paper and handed it to Emma. "It's just a formality. One of your parents should probably read and sign it."

"Yes, it needs to be someone over eighteen," Ms. Strickland said. "We have a holiday arts and crafts fair every year, but I think one around Mother's Day is a wonderful idea. We can certainly help you promote it as well."

"Oh, okay," Emma said. "Thanks. That sounds . . . great."

I wanted to ask her if Mr. Dooney had told her why we wanted to have the fair. Did she know it was because her son wanted to kick the bookmobile off the grocery store's parking lot? It seemed like if she knew, she wouldn't have been so eager to help us.

"Can I get you girls that lemonade now?" Mr. Dooney asked.

"Actually," I said, "I can't stay. I just remembered that I need to get home. Sorry."

"Yeah, me, too," Emma said. She waved the application in the air. "Thanks for this. We'll read it over and make a decision soon."

"Oh, do you have other options, then?" Ms. Strickland asked.

"Um, yeah, we just have a lot to think over," Emma said. "Thanks again. Bye!"

She turned around and almost ran out the front door, and Carmen and I scurried after her.

Emma walked straight for the beach and didn't stop until we were practically to the ocean. I zipped up my jacket because it was breezy. The fresh air felt good, though.

"What is going on?" Carmen asked. "One minute you're ready to have vanilla wafers and lemonade and the next minute you're running out of there like . . . like Vincent van Gogh just called and asked to meet for pizza."

"I wish!" I said.

"I can't believe it," Emma said as she kicked at a stick in the sand. "Of all the people he could have asked, it had to be her?"

"Who is she?" Carmen asked. "Please, tell me."

"Her last name is Strickland," I said. "Remember Mr. Strickland, the terrible manager of the grocery store? That's her son."

Carmen said, "Oh. Ohhhh! Wow. I thought the name sounded familiar, I just couldn't remember where I'd heard it. So, what do we do now?"

"Seems pretty obvious to me," I said. "There's no way this will work. We need to come up with a new idea."

"No," Emma said. "I don't think so. You know why? She might listen to us. She might love to read, we don't know, and if she does, she might agree with us and not her son. Who knows, maybe she could even get him to change his mind." She smiled. "You guys, I'm just realizing this might be the best thing that could happen to us."

I couldn't believe what I was hearing. How could they think this would work? I mean, this wasn't some random dude she knew. This was her son. Why would she ever take our side?

"Should we go back there?" Carmen asked. "Talk to her?"

"You guys," I said. "What is happening right now? She's his *mom*."

"But sometimes children make mistakes, right?" Emma said. "If we can get her to see that he's making a really big one, she might help us." Emma stopped and stared at me for a second before she continued. "Wait a second. You're not using this as an excuse, are you?"

"What do you mean?" I asked.

"Like, this could be a way out for you," Emma said. "So you don't have to figure out how to find the courage to put your work out there. Well, too bad. We're not giving up yet. Right, Carmen?"

"Um, I'm not sure," Carmen said, cracking her knuckles nervously. "I can see both of your points, you know?"

Emma started walking. "Stay if you want. We'll never know unless we ask."

Carmen looked at me, her eyes begging me to go along, too. But I couldn't do it.

"Sorry," she said as she ran past me to join Emma.

I turned around and faced the ocean so I wouldn't have to watch them walking away from me. I took in a deep breath of the salty sea air as I watched the giant waves roll in the distance and the frothy tide spill toward me. The gray cloudy sky matched how I felt on the inside.

Was Emma right? Was I using this as a way out? Was my fear so big it was covering my brain like a giant tarp and I couldn't see anything clearly?

I had no idea. All I knew was that I felt as broken and alone as the empty crab shell at my feet.

Reasons I don't like fighting with friends

* *It makes me feel sick.*
* *It feels like the world is ending.*
* *It's hard to know what to do after the fight. Like, who's supposed to say sorry when you both think you're right?*
* *It's about as fun as cleaning the bathroom. Except I'd rather clean the bathroom.*
* *I think I'd rather do almost anything else. Anything.*

Sixteen

BEST EVER

When I got home, Miranda was in the kitchen, getting stuff out of the cupboards, like she was about to bake something.

"Can I help?" I asked.

"Sure," she said.

"What are we making?"

"A cake."

"What for?"

"Um . . . for me? And you?"

"What happened to training?" I asked. "Aren't you supposed to be staying fit and healthy for your tryouts?"

Junior lifeguard tryouts were coming up in May. I don't know why I was questioning her, though. It's not like I wanted to talk her out of making a cake. Why would I do that? What was I thinking? Actually, I wasn't thinking. Heartbreak will do that to you.

"I'll work it off tomorrow with the girls," she replied. "We're swimming all day."

I looked at the recipe on the counter and saw that it was called "The Best Chocolate Cake Recipe (Ever)." It looked like she'd printed it off the internet.

"You know someone could make the worst cake ever and simply call it the best cake ever, right?"

"It has hundreds of comments and a five-star rating," she said. "Even if it's not the best, it'll be good. Good enough for me, anyway. If you don't want any, fine with me."

"No, I want some," I said as I read through the ingredient list and started pulling things out the cupboards. "Chocolate makes everything better, right?"

"Uh-oh. What's going on?"

"Um, I don't see espresso powder. Do we even need that? Will it make the cake taste like coffee?"

"No, it wouldn't make it taste like coffee. It's supposed to make the cake super flavorful or something. We can skip it, though. But you didn't answer my question. What happened?"

I set the vanilla, baking soda, and baking powder on the counter and then turned around. "I got in a fight with Emma and Carmen."

"Oh. That's all?" Miranda asked as she got back to work, measuring out two cups each of flour and sugar. "Okay, so tell me. What happened?"

I hesitated for a second. After all, sisters are masters at

telling you that you're wrong, and I really didn't need to hear that. But who else was I going to talk to about it? So, I told her the whole story.

When I finished, she said, "Well, Pooh, you know what I'm going to ask you, right?" She poured the wet ingredients into the dry ingredients, and while she held the bowl, I scraped the sides with a spatula.

"No. What?"

She gave me a look. "Oh, come on. You know. Do you want to sell your paintings at the fair or not? Be honest."

"Well, no, but—"

She stopped me. "Okay, so, there is more going on than just being worried about Ms. Strickland. You should probably think about whether your friends are right, even if you don't want to admit that." She set the bowl down and grabbed the handheld mixer. "Can you spray the cake pans, then put the parchment paper in them?"

While she mixed, I got the pans ready. When she was done, she handed me one of the beaters to lick. "Mmmm," she said as she tasted the batter. "Good, right?"

"Really good," I told her.

As we stood there eating the batter we probably shouldn't have been eating because of possible salmonella poisoning, I decided to see if my older and wiser sister had any advice.

"How do I do it?" I asked.

"Do what?"

"Put myself out there? I'm just . . . I'm so afraid."

"Oh, Pooh," Miranda said, leaning up against the counter after she threw her beater in the sink. "I can't tell you how to do it. Courage isn't something you can turn on and off like a light switch. All I know is, yeah, I might not pass the junior lifeguard test, but how do I know if I don't try? Maybe I won't pass, but I work hard not to focus on that because all it does is make me feel like garbage. I focus on what it will feel like when I pass and all the good things that'll come after that.

"Instead of thinking about all the bad things that might happen, can you think about the good things that might happen instead? I mean, you might sell a bunch of paintings and be able to give a lot of money to the Buttons. Think about that. Wouldn't that feel incredible?"

"Yes, but—"

She cut me off again. "No. No buts. Like, don't tell me that won't happen. Because you have no idea what's going to happen. Unless you have some secret powers you've been hiding from me this entire time."

It made me smile. If only I had some secret powers. The ability to fly. Or to be invisible. Or to speed-read books but still understand everything. I could read so many more books that way.

"Nope. No secret powers," I told her.

She went to work pouring the batter into the pans. "Then you just have to power through like the rest of us. You know what you need to do?"

"No, Miranda. I have no idea. That's why I'm talking to you about this. So you can *help* me."

She opened the oven door and carefully placed the cake pans on the middle rack. "Every time you start the negative talk in your head, pretend it's your best friend saying those things out loud. Would you let her get away with that? Would you let her beat herself up like that?"

"Probably not," I said softly.

"More like, *definitely* not," my sister said. "So you shouldn't do that to yourself either."

Why was that so hard to do? I wondered.

She set the timer and then pulled me into a hug. "Try and remember something, okay? When people do hard things, it's not because they're not afraid. It's because they're afraid but *they do them anyway*. That's what bravery is."

I knew exactly what she was saying. I needed to do the hard thing.

"I'm going to go paint for a while," I told her. "Can we have pizza for dinner before we have cake for dessert?"

"Sounds good to me," she said. "I'll check with Mom and make sure it's okay."

I started to walk away and then turned around. "Miranda?"

"Yeah?"

"Thanks. I kind of knew you would probably tell me I was wrong, but you were actually pretty nice about it."

"Am I the best big sister *ever*?" she teased.

I turned around and headed toward my room. "If you say so, the internet will probably believe it!"

Good things that might happen from selling my paintings

* *I'll raise money to help Mr. and Mrs. Button.*
* *I'll raise my confidence level.*
* *A kid gets a painting of a cute owl for a birthday gift.*
* *People go home and try to paint their own owls (or trees or cats or cupcakes).*
* *Little kids are inspired to be artists someday.*
* *More art in the world = a better world.*

Seventeen

HERE, KITTY, KITTY

Last fall, we had spirit week at my old school. On crazy hair day, I used a bunch of Miranda's ponytail holders to make little twists all over my head. I added some neon-pink and green pipe cleaners to make it bright and colorful, then sprayed a lot of hairspray to help keep everything in place. I looked awesome, if I do say so myself, in a crazy hair kind of way. But when I left for school, the bathroom was a disaster area. I just didn't have time to clean it. Well, Miranda went ballistic after school that day. She was super mad I used her stuff without asking and that I didn't clean up my mess.

After she finished screaming at me, I apologized, but she didn't speak to me for three long days. Because we live together, it was almost impossible for it to go on much longer than that. And, you know, we're sisters. That's what sisters do. They get upset with each other. They use the silent treatment masterfully. And then they make up and become best friends again.

I knew I needed to apologize to Emma and Carmen. Saying "I'm sorry" wasn't the hard part, though. The hard part would be what came after that—going to the arts and crafts fair to sell my paintings. Because an apology isn't just empty words. Or it shouldn't be anyway. It should be followed by doing something that shows you really mean it. Like, I haven't touched my sister's hair stuff again without asking first, even if I think she's being kind of a diva about the whole thing.

Admitting you're wrong is hard. Working to make things right? Even harder. But I wanted to try.

After a breakfast of a banana and a slice of the very delicious chocolate cake (I figured it counted as breakfast because of the eggs), I was about to head over to Emma's when there was a knock at the door. Miranda had already left for the day and Mom was in the bathroom, so I went to the window to see who it was. My heart did a little cartwheel when I saw Carmen and Oscar standing there. She held a folded-up blanket and Oscar had a couple of plastic buckets with some small sand tools sticking out of them.

"Hi, Juliet," Carmen said when I opened the door. "Hope it's not too early."

"No, it's fine," I said. "I'm so happy to see you. Do you want to come in?"

"Actually, we were wondering if you'd like to go to the beach with us? He can build a castle and we can maybe, um, talk?"

I smiled. "Ooh, yeah, I'd love to. Just let me get my hoodie. Be right back."

I ran and grabbed my favorite purple sweatshirt and threw it on. "Going to the beach with Carmen," I yelled as I flew past the closed bathroom door.

"Okay," Mom replied. "Have fun."

If Carmen had come to see me and wanted to talk, it meant that she wasn't *too* mad at me. I couldn't deny I was curious about what had happened after they'd gone back to talk to Ms. Strickland. Hopefully Carmen would tell me things were good and we could move forward with the arts and crafts fair.

As we made our way to the beach, the sun out and the sky such a bright blue it made me feel like I was walking inside a gorgeous painting, Oscar asked about our cat. I figured he must have seen him behind me when I'd opened the door.

"His name is Casper," I told him. "Like the ghost. It was a TV show. My sister and I watched it when we were little because it was one of my dad's favorite shows when he was a kid."

"Does Casper stay inside all the time, or does he go outside?" Oscar asked, swinging his buckets as he walked.

"He stays inside," I said. "At our old house, he'd go into our fenced backyard sometimes and lie in the sun. But here, it's just safer for him to stay in the house."

"I bet he misses his old home," he said. "Does he seem sad?"

I looked at Carmen and she just kind of shrugged, like, "Kids are funny, right?"

"He might, but I don't think he's too sad. The first week, he hid sometimes. He was probably nervous about being in a new place. But now he seems okay."

"In case you can't tell, it's not just me who wishes we could have a pet," Carmen said.

"Yeah, I'm sorry that you can't have one. Have you ever tried to build an animal out of sand?" I asked him.

"Nope," he said. "Have you?"

"My sister and I did a sea turtle," I told him. "It was really hard."

"Did you take a picture?" he asked.

While Carmen threw down the blanket, I pulled out my phone and showed him the photo. "That's really good," he said. "Maybe I'll try and make a cat. Just the head, though. The body might be too hard."

"Sounds good," I said. "I can help, too, if you want."

"Maybe," he said. "I'll let you know."

I knew that was his nice way of saying he wanted to do it by himself. For now.

I sat on the plaid wool blanket across from Carmen. She had a faded pink baseball cap on that said GIRL POWER.

I took a deep breath before I said, "Carmen, I'm really sorry about yesterday."

"It's okay," she said.

"No, it's not. I jumped when I saw the chance to find a different way to raise money because I was thinking about myself. And that was wrong. I've decided I'm going to sell my paintings at the fair."

"You are?" she asked. "Because, honestly, you don't have to."

"I just think . . ." I paused. "I don't want to be so afraid that I miss out. Maybe I won't get many paintings done and maybe my stuff won't sell, but maybe . . . well, maybe it will all be fine, like you and Emma keep saying. I really want to help Mr. and Mrs. Button and the bookmobile. That's what I want to focus on."

She looked at her brother, working hard, digging in the sand. Then she leaned in. "I wish I could figure out what to focus on so I'm not so afraid all the time. Almost every night I wish on all the stars and hope things change."

It hurt my heart to hear her say that she was afraid. But I didn't have any ideas on how she could change that. It was so different from my own situation. And honestly, it made me feel like my problems were tiny grains of sand compared to her giant-pieces-of-driftwood problems. Then

I remembered what my mom told me. Sometimes people just need a friend to listen.

"I want to help, but I don't really know what to do," I told her. "I'm always here if you want to talk, though."

She smiled. "Thanks. That means a lot."

"So, what happened with Ms. Strickland?" I asked. "Did she say she'd still help with the fair after you told her why we wanted to have it?"

"The conversation was kind of . . . strange," Carmen said, picking up a handful of sand and letting it slowly slip through her fingers. "She said she wanted to think about it, and she'd get back to us."

"Hm. Do you think that means she wants to talk to her son about it?"

"Maybe. Mr. Dooney seemed to be on our side. I have a feeling it's going to be okay. I don't know why I think that, exactly, I just do."

"Hey, can you guys come help me?" Oscar called out.

He'd drawn a big circle with two triangles at the top. Then he was dumping sand into the outlined area, trying to make it three-dimensional. Basically, he was trying to do the same thing we'd done with the turtle's shell when Miranda and I had made a sea turtle in the sand. But instead of a simple shell, he was going to try to make it look like a cat's face.

"What do you want us to do?" Carmen asked.

"Make it look like a cat," he said. "It's a lot harder than I thought."

I stepped over and kneeled down next to him. "Let's smooth out this sand as best we can and then we'll go to work drawing the nose, mouth, and whiskers. That will make it look more like a cat, I think."

"Okay," he said with a grin. "Thanks!"

As we all worked together, I knew this was what Mom had meant when she'd said there were things I could do for them even if I couldn't solve all their problems. Making a cat in the sand was difficult, but not impossible. I'd help until Oscar was happy with it. Sure, there were lots of things I couldn't do, but this was something I *could* do, and I was so glad about that.

Reasons Carmen's mom should be allowed to stay

* *She's a mom to two children who were born here.*
* *She just wants to make a nice life for her family.*
* *She's not doing anything to hurt people.*
* *Carmen and Oscar have to live without their dad; they shouldn't have to live without their mom, too.*
* *Kids shouldn't be punished because adults have some weird idea of what "safety" means.*
* *The United States is a country made up of immigrants. Why does it seem like so many people have forgotten that?*

Eighteen

ANIMALS EVERYWHERE

We spent hours on the cat. Lots and lots of people stopped, took photos, and complimented us on our mad skills. By the time we were done, it was a made-of-sand masterpiece. Oscar was so proud. I took photos with my phone and told him I'd print them out and give them to him so he could remember it forever.

The sad thing was, when it was time for them to go home, Oscar didn't want to leave his cat, which he'd named Sandy.

"She'll miss me," Oscar said.

"She's not real, bro," Carmen said. "Come on. It's way past lunchtime and I'm starving."

"But—"

Carmen shook her head. "Nope. Time to go."

I stood up and tried to brush the sand off my pants, but it was a lost cause.

"What are you going to do now?" Oscar asked me. I think he was hoping I'd say that I'd find a wizard who could turn the cat made of sand into a real cat and make his biggest wish come true. But of course, I couldn't say that.

"I'm going to go see our friend Emma," I said. "I have something I need to talk to her about. After that, I'll go home and make something to eat. Probably a pickle and turkey sandwich."

Oscar gently brushed his hand over one of the cat's ears. "I'll never forget you, Sandy."

"Is your mom allergic to cats?" I asked, thinking about Emma and the reason she couldn't have one.

"No," Carmen said. "I think she just worries about the cost."

"You want me to paint you a picture of a cat?" I asked Oscar. "I can do any color you want. Then you could hang it in your room."

He stood up and rubbed his hands together, trying to get rid of the sand. "It's not the same as having a real one, though." Then he shrugged and said, "But . . . okay. Can you do a gray one?"

"Yep. I'll do one tonight, after dinner."

"We really love the beach one she did for us, right, Oscar?" Carmen asked.

"You mean the one that *I'm* in and you're *not*?" he teased. "It's all right, I guess."

I laughed. Carmen rolled her eyes, like, "Oh, brother." Literally. "Thanks, dude," I said. "I'm honored."

"See you later," Carmen said as she grabbed Oscar's hand and gently pulled him toward the boardwalk. "Hope it goes okay with Emma."

"Me, too," I said. "Bye!"

As I walked down the boardwalk toward Emma's house, I could see Ms. Strickland and Mr. Dooney outside on his patio. She was at his house? Again? I noticed he was dressed a little nicer than he usually was, in a short-sleeved dress shirt and slacks and no cap on his head for once. She wore another pretty skirt, this time with little birds all over it.

"Hello, Mr. Dooney," I said when I approached them. "And hi, Ms. Strickland."

"Hello, Juliet," Mr. Dooney replied. "How are you on this fine Saturday?"

"I'm all right, I guess," I said. I looked at Ms. Strickland. "I'm sorry I didn't come back yesterday with Emma and Carmen to talk to you. About why we want to have the arts and crafts fair."

"It's perfectly fine," she said. "They explained the situation to me very well. And I've decided to move ahead with the fair because I truly think it's a wonderful idea."

I was kind of shocked. She was really going to take our side? "But what about your son? Did you talk to him about it?"

"No, I haven't," she said. "I thought about it but decided I wanted to make up my own mind without his influence. The way I see it, he told the Buttons they could pay rent and keep the bookmobile in its spot, and so there's nothing wrong with me playing a small part in helping to do that."

I didn't want to talk her out of it. I really didn't. But I also thought she should know the whole story. "He told Emma's dad he was hoping to put a hot dog stand in its place. So I think he's hoping they'll move it somewhere else. Does that . . . change your mind?"

She wrinkled her nose. "A hot dog stand? Oh, my. That's a terrible idea, if I do say so myself. You girls should get that application filled out as soon as possible so we can get to work. Okay?"

I nodded. "Okay. I'm going to see Emma now. If you're going to be here for a little while, we can probably bring it back this afternoon."

"We're going for a walk on the beach now," Mr. Dooney said. He looked at his watch. "How about if we meet up here at two o'clock? That gives you an hour or so."

"Sounds good." I started to walk away but then I stopped. "Mr. Dooney, can I ask you something?"

"Of course you may," he said.

"Were you ever scared that people wouldn't like the stories you wrote?" I asked.

"All the time," he said. "But you know what I told myself?"

"What?"

"As long as you're trying, you're not failing. Failing is if you don't try at all. Does that make sense?"

"I think so."

"Are you a writer?" he asked.

"No. Just an artist," I said. "Or, I want to be, anyway."

"If you're making art, you're an artist," Ms. Strickland said with a smile. "It's as simple as that, really. And if you don't mind, I have a bit of advice for you, too. I love making my own clothes, like this skirt, and sometimes I'll worry about whether everyone will like it or not. But then I remember, it doesn't matter if everyone likes it. All that matters is that I like it! Who cares about the rest of them?" She winked at me. "Draw or paint for yourself. Do it because it makes you happy. And I bet if it makes you happy, it'll make other people happy. Not everyone, of course, but you'll find your people. You'll see."

"Thanks," I said. "See you back here in a little while."

When I got to Emma's house, Emma, her dad, and her brother Lance were all outside. Emma was kneeling on the pavement, petting a scruffy brown dog. It didn't have a collar and wasn't on a leash.

"Hey, Juliet," Emma's dad, Rick, said. "You wouldn't happen to know where this sweet boy belongs, do you?"

"I found him on the boardwalk all by himself," Lance said.

I glanced at Emma but she was focused on the dog. I

wanted her to look at me. To say something or smile and let me know we were okay.

"No, sorry," I told them. "Never seen him before."

"Can we keep him, Dad?" Emma asked. "Please? I'll do all the work of taking care of him. I promise."

"Honey," Rick said. "You know we can't do that. He belongs to someone, and that someone is probably really missing him right now. Come on, let's get him in the car so I can take him to the shelter. They can check to see if he has a chip."

"If he doesn't, what happens to him?" Emma asked.

"He'll stay at the shelter and hopefully his family will look there when they can't find him," her dad replied.

"Hopefully?" Emma said. "What if they don't? What will happen to him?"

"Let's not worry about that right now," Rick said. "One thing at a time. He might have a chip and everything will be fine."

Emma leaned in, wrapped her arms tightly around the dog, and buried her face into his neck. Lance walked over, leaned down, and whispered something in Emma's ear. After that, she let go and Lance picked up the dog and carried him to the car.

"You girls want to go?" her dad asked.

I waved the application in the air. "Emma, I have news. About the fair? We're supposed to meet up with Mr. Dooney in an hour."

"Oh, okay," she said. "We'll stay here, then. But, Lance, will you text me and let me know what happens?"

"Yeah, sure," he said as got into the car.

Emma watched them drive away. When they were gone, she finally turned to me. "I wish we could have kept him."

"I know," I said. "I'm sorry." I paused. "And not just about the dog. I'm sorry about yesterday. You were right, I was using Ms. Strickland as an excuse. But I've decided I'm going to set a goal of doing two paintings a day and sell my paintings at the fair, which we get to have at the senior center because I just talked to her."

"Really?" she asked quietly, clapping her hands together. "It's really going to happen?"

"Yep. I even told her about the hot dog stand idea, to make sure she didn't want to support that instead, but she said the bookmobile is a much better thing to have in the parking lot."

"So what happens now?" Emma asked.

"We need to fill out the application and then take it to her at two o'clock," I said. "We'll need an adult to sign it. Is your mom home?"

"She's at the ice cream shop, but we can walk over there and have her sign it." She smiled. "And get a cone while we're at it."

My stomach gurgled at the thought of ice cream. I hadn't had lunch yet and I was hungry. Cake for breakfast and ice cream for lunch? This was turning out to be a very good day!

As we went inside, I told her about building a sand kitty with Oscar and Carmen. "They both want a cat really bad," I said.

"I know the feeling," Emma said. "I guess we'll just have to come over to your house all the time and love on Casper. He won't mind, will he?"

"For the first ten seconds, no, he won't," I told her. "But after that, your guess is as good as mine. Since you've never had one, you might not know that cats can be kind of, um, moody?"

She smiled. "Hey, just like me! I love cats even more now."

I laughed. "Right—easy to say before one tries to scratch your eyes out."

Reasons I wish I could give Carmen and Oscar a cat

* *A pet can help you feel better when you're sad.*
* *Lots of animals need love and Carmen and Oscar have some to give.*
* *Cat snuggles are the very best.*
* *Those two deserve something happy in their life.*
* *They'd be the purr-fect cat owners, I'm sure of it.*

Nineteen

SURPRISES GALORE

Once our application was accepted, we got busy. The fair was scheduled for the Saturday before Mother's Day, coming up in a couple of weeks. Ms. Strickland made flyers, and Carmen, Emma, and I helped put them up around town. You should have seen Mrs. Button's face when we told her about the fair. She could hardly believe we were doing it to help save the bookmobile.

"How will I ever be able to repay you girls?" she asked with tears in her eyes.

"You're here almost every day with free books," Emma said. "What else could we ask for?"

Every night, I painted at least one picture, sometimes two. Mom pitched in some money and helped me buy thirty small canvases. I figured if I could come up with twenty-five paintings that I was happy with and charged ten dollars a painting, I'd make two hundred and fifty dollars. I could donate half of that to the Buttons, pay Mom fifty dollars for the canvases, and still have some money left over for myself.

But that meant I had to work fast. Not only that, I could only throw out five paintings I wasn't happy with. I promised myself I wouldn't make any decisions until I had done all thirty. And even then, I wouldn't decide on my own; I'd ask my family or friends for their opinions. Unless I really messed up and couldn't stand the thought of showing something to anyone.

And that's what happened with the very first painting. I'd had this brilliant idea to paint a tree with a little girl sitting under it, reading a book. I thought if I had the girl holding a book in such a way that her face was naturally covered, it wouldn't be too hard. But I was wrong. It looked like the poor girl was suffering from some terrible disease that caused her fingers to swell up like sausages.

When I got brave enough to show my sister the ugly thing, she told me, "Keep it simple, Pooh. Do the things you love to do and do well. Like owls. People love owls, I'm telling you. You could probably do thirty cute and colorful owls and you'd sell out in an hour."

"That's banana pants," I told her.

"No, it's not," she replied. "It's called being optimistic. You should try it sometime." Then she'd waved her hands in front of me like she was casting a spell. "Believe, Juliet. You can do it. *Believe*."

I remembered how I'd said that to her before we'd gone

to Dad's apartment for the first time. It hadn't worked then; why should it work now?

Still, I thought about what she'd said. My list of favorite things to paint has six things on it: the night sky, owls, trees, cats, cupcakes, and flowers. So I stuck to those. And my sister was right—by painting the things I was good at, I didn't have any more disasters. And painting went a lot faster since I had my process down, although every day I grew more and more nervous I wouldn't have enough to display in a booth all to myself.

My favorite painting was a gray cat like I'd given to Oscar, except this time, I painted a red-and-white checkered collar around his neck. When I paint cats, I do them from behind, like sitting on a windowsill looking outside, so I don't have to try to get their eyes, nose, and mouth exactly right. The little bit of color on the collar really made the piece super adorable for some reason.

Before I was able to finish all my paintings, I had to take a break for the weekend because we went to see Dad again. I thought about taking my art supplies with me, but it would have been a lot to manage, so I told myself when I got home, I'd just have to work three times as hard.

When we arrived at Dad's place, with a Tony's pizza and some side salads in hand again, he said, "Do you want to see your rooms now or after we eat?"

"Silly question," I said as I glanced at Miranda. "Right?"

"Now!" she said as she dashed toward her room. I did

the same. I had expected it to be pretty basic, with a bed and a nightstand and maybe a small dresser. But Dad had gone above and beyond, because I had a bookcase filled with books. As I skimmed the titles, I was pretty impressed that he'd gotten a nice mix of classics and contemporaries. All of them had stickers on the front, like he'd bought them at a garage sale, but I didn't mind. I loved that he'd made the effort to get me something for my room that he knew I'd like.

"What do you think?" he asked from the doorway.

I turned around and studied the room a little more. The bedspread wasn't very exciting—just plain navy blue, but on the floor, at the foot of the bed, was the best rug I'd ever seen. It was covered in bright, colorful owls.

"The rug is my favorite," I said. "And the bookcase, too. I can't believe you even went and bought some books for me."

"Well, I want it to feel like your second home. Eventually. I mean, I know it'll take time, but hopefully having things you like will help."

I went over and gave him a hug. "Thanks, Dad."

"You're welcome."

Miranda came in just then and gave him a hug as well. "I'm impressed," she said. "Everything looks amazing. I love that you got me a vanity so Juliet and I don't have to fight over getting ready in the bathroom like we do at home."

"Did you put everything together yourself?" I asked.

He laughed. "Oh, no. I had help from some friends. It took us about a day to get it all done. We listened to music and I fed them well. It was a pretty fun day."

We went to the kitchen table and took our seats. As we put dressing on our salads, Dad said, "It's supposed to be nice and warm tomorrow. Want to go to a new park across town and have a picnic? Toss a Frisbee around?"

I glanced at Miranda, and when I did, she gave me a little eyebrow raise. I think we were both thinking the same thing—*Dad actually has plans!*

"Can we make cookies again tomorrow morning to take along?" Miranda asked.

He shook his head. "No. Absolutely not." Then he grinned. "Are you kidding? When have I ever said no to cookies?"

"Miranda," I said, "I just had the best idea. Could you make some cookies for my booth at the arts and craft fair? Maybe I could do an incentive, like buy a painting, get two free cookies."

"You're not going to need cookies to sell your paintings, Pooh," she replied.

"Juliet, that reminds me. I want you to know, I'm planning on coming," Dad said.

I had told him about the fair on the phone when we'd talked last, but I'd never imagined he might want to come.

"You don't have to," I said.

"I know, but I want to," he said. "This is a big deal and I want to be there to support you."

"That's nice of you, but . . ."

"But what?" he asked. His face drooped. "You don't want me to come?"

"No," I said. "It's not that, it's just . . . I may not sell anything. Like, it could be a total failure."

"It won't be a total failure," he said. "How could it be? Your art is really good, and you've been working at it for a long time."

"I know, but there's no guarantee," I said.

"There never is," he said. "That's life. You do your best and see what happens. Anyway, none of that matters and I want to be there. Okay?"

"Okay."

He smiled. "Good."

We started eating our salads and then Miranda's phone buzzed. "I'm going to eat and then hang out with April for a while, if that's okay," she told us.

"Sure," Dad said. He looked at me. "Inca around this weekend?"

"No," I said. "She's in Santa Monica with her family."

Dad grabbed some plates and dished up slices of pizza for us. "I'm sorry you won't get to see her."

"Maybe next time," I said.

"Want me to ask her if she'd like to come along with me to the fair?" Dad asked.

"No," I said. "That's a long way to go just to see my little booth. And it might get boring, hanging out there for hours."

"Well, think on it some more," Dad said. "You might change your mind. And if you do, I'm happy to help get her there if I can."

"Can you help get *me* there?" I asked.

He looked at me, confused. "What do you mean?"

"She's nervous, that's all," Miranda said.

Ten more paintings to go. And then I had to cross my fingers that twenty-five people would be interested in buying art made by an eleven-year-old.

"If it makes you feel any better," Dad said, "the zoo has started having certain animals walk through paint and then they sell those paintings to the public. They sell out every time we offer them. The ones by the raccoons are especially popular."

That did not make me feel better. Actually, whoever came up with that idea was a genius. If I didn't hate lying so much, I could tell people that my paintings were done by squirrel monkeys, deep in the tropical rain forest. Whether they were gorgeous or super-duper ugly, it wouldn't matter. They'd sell out for sure.

If only I could sell artwork done by

* Mermaids
* Unicorns
* Aliens
* Fairies
* Superheroes
* Leprechauns
* Wizards
* Witches
* Bigfoot
* Vincent van Gogh

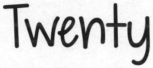

Twenty

PETS ARE THE BEST

When I got home Sunday evening, I was getting ready to do a load of laundry when Emma texted me.

> You're not going to believe this. No one has claimed the dog, so we may get to bring him home.

I texted back: That's so exciting! But what about the allergies?

She replied: Dad thinks it might be part poodle, which means it could be hypoallergenic. He and my brother didn't have an allergic reaction to the dog when they took him to the shelter. Anyway, we're going to go after school tomorrow and make sure. Wanna go with us?

I told her I'd love to and then went back to collecting laundry from my mom and my sister. Mom was in her bed, reading a book with Casper curled up next to her. She looked up when I came in.

"Oh, thanks, Juju Bean," she said as she set her book

down. "If you'd like, I can put the clothes in the dryer so you don't have to wait up."

"It's not that late," I told her as I set the basket down and sat on the edge of the bed to pet Casper. "I was going to do a painting before I go to bed anyway."

"Are you sure?" Mom asked. "It's a school night."

"We all slept in this morning, so I'm not that tired. Besides, I don't have much time left, Mom."

"It's going to be fine," she said.

"Hopefully." I paused. "You know, this whole thing is weird."

"What? What do you mean?"

"I mean, part of my brain screams at me to work faster and make more paintings. Make as many as I can because the more I have, the more I can sell. But the other part of my brain screams that none of it matters anyway because I'm not going to sell a single one."

"Honey, you'll sell some. I know you will. You're too talented not to."

I rolled my eyes. "Okay, whatever. You're my mom. Of course you're going to say that.

"But it's true," she said. "You'll see."

"Yep. We'll see."

She smiled. "Your dad texted me and said you guys had a really nice time this weekend. That makes me happy. With time, everything gets easier, doesn't it?"

"I guess so. Oh, I just remembered, can I go with Emma and her dad to the animal shelter tomorrow after school? They found a stray dog a few weeks ago and no one's claimed it, so they might adopt it."

"Wow," she said. "That's exciting. Yes, that's fine. Just don't get any ideas, okay?" Now she started petting Casper. He's pretty much irresistible that way. "Not sure our favorite kitty would like sharing our house with another four-legged friend."

"I don't want a dog, but you know what I wish I could do?"

"What?"

"I wish I could bring home a cat for Carmen and Oscar. They really want one. I guess their mom worries about the cost, though."

Mom nodded. "It's one more mouth to feed, sweetie. Even if it's a tiny mouth. And on top of the daily care, there are veterinary visits, too, for vaccinations and all those other necessary things it takes to keep an animal healthy. It's nice that she's thought about it and knows it's not a good decision for their family right now. Some people jump in without thinking things through and that's how shelters get so overcrowded with animals no one wants."

I stood up. "But that's the thing, Mom. There are so many animals that need homes. Isn't there something we can do? Some way we can help them? You're a vet, it seems like you should be able to think of something."

She kept petting Casper and he started purring. It was

one of my favorite sounds in the world. I went over to her hamper and threw her clothes into the laundry basket. "Hm. I don't know," she said. "Let me think on it, okay? And if you come up with any ideas, I'm all ears."

I used to hate it when my mom or dad said they needed time to think about something. It always seemed like it was just a way to put off saying no for a while longer. But now I understood that sometimes decisions aren't easy, and taking time to make them is a smart thing to do. Ms. Strickland took time to think about the arts and crafts fair and I had been sure she'd tell us she didn't want to do it, but then the opposite had happened.

Maybe my mom or I would come up with some brilliant idea so that Oscar and Carmen could have a cat of their very own. It wouldn't solve their problems, I knew that. But having a cat to cuddle might make those problems more bearable.

Reasons shelters are the best place to get a pet

* *There are usually lots of animals to choose from.*
* *Every single animal needs a good home and someone to love.*
* *The animals didn't ask to be there and how sad is it that they have to live in a small kennel day after day with no real home to call their own?*
* *My mom told me that puppies at pet stores are often from puppy mills where dogs are made to breed over and over again and often live in bad conditions.*
* *Adult pets are often already trained—so much easier than having to train a puppy or a kitten.*
* *An animal from a shelter costs a lot less money than one from a pet store or a breeder.*

Twenty-One

SHELTER FRIENDS

The scruffy dog we'd seen a few weeks ago didn't look quite so scruffy anymore. They'd given him a bath and brushed him. Maybe they did that in hopes of helping to get him adopted more quickly.

"Is there any way to know what kind he is?" Rick asked the volunteer, Shelly, who had brought the dog out to a meet-and-greet spot the shelter had for this kind of thing. All of the volunteers wore blue vests with a name tag; that's how I knew her name.

"We had a veterinarian examine him after you brought him in," Shelly said as she read notes on a clipboard she held. "He's in excellent health, has been neutered, no chip, as you already know, and we believe he's a labradoodle, approximately four years old."

"A cross between a Lab and a poodle?" Emma's dad asked.

"That's correct," Shelly said.

Emma kneeled down and the dog wiggled its way to her, where he tried to kiss her face over and over again. Emma squealed as she tried to keep her face away from his tongue while attempting to pet him. The dog seemed to really love her.

"Oh, Dad," Emma said as she plopped onto the floor with her legs out in front of her, allowing the dog to jump into her lap. "Can we take him home? Please?"

Lance sat down next to Emma. The dog immediately went to him and tried to give him a bunch of love just like he'd done with Emma.

"I can't believe no one came looking for him," Emma said. "He seems so sweet."

"It's hard to know what might have happened," Shelly said. "Sometimes people have to move and they can't take their pets with them. Sometimes a dog runs away from a bad living situation and the owners don't care enough to go looking for him. It's just hard to say."

While Emma and Lance continued their lovefest with their four-legged friend, I figured this was my chance to find out more about the cats at the shelter. "How many cats do you have right now?"

"I'm not sure of the exact number," Shelly said, "but over twenty. Are you looking to adopt one?"

"Not for me, but I have a friend who might be

interested," I said. "Would it be all right . . . I mean, can I see them, please?"

Shelly turned to Emma's dad. "You folks okay here by yourselves for a few minutes?"

"Absolutely," Rick said. "We'll take good care of him."

Shelly handed Rick the leash and then told me to follow her. We walked down a short hallway and then she opened a door that led into a big room with cages all along the walls. There was another lady with a blue vest holding a black cat and talking to it.

"That's Midnight," Shelly said, gesturing at the cat. "He's a staff favorite. Such a lovebug."

"And I'm Mel," the lady holding Midnight said. "Are you looking for a cat for your family?"

"No," I said. "We already have one. A friend of mine might be interested, though. Do you have any gray ones?"

"We sure do," Mel said, pointing to a cage close to her. "Right over here. We often don't know what their names were before they came to us. We call this fine gentleman Dexter."

I went over to peek in on him. He was curled up on a small blanket and I wanted so badly to reach in and pet him. I think Shelly read my mind. She unlatched the cage door for me and said, "Go ahead and pet him if you'd like. He's a nice one. Not all of them are, sadly. Makes it a lot harder to find them a home. After all, no one wants to take home a cat who acts like he wants to shred you to pieces when you try to pet him."

"Hi, Dexter," I said softly as I stuck my hand in and gently scratched the top of his head in between his ears. He woke up and lifted his head with a small "Mew."

"How long as he been here?" I asked.

"About a month or so?" Shelly said. "I think? A family found him out in the country, wandering around on their property. He was really skinny. Someone probably dropped him off out there. That happens a lot."

"That's so sad," I said.

Dexter stretched out his front legs, yawned, and then stood up, leaning into my hand as he did. I wanted so much to scoop him up into my arms and say, "I'll take him!" And then knock on Carmen's door and say, "Surprise!" I could just imagine Carmen and Oscar, jumping up and down and squealing with excitement. They'd be happier than a fat cat sleeping near a window on a sunny day. But as much as I wanted to do that, I knew I couldn't, because it wasn't up to me. Their mom had said no, simple as that.

I pulled my arm out and turned to Shelly. "Thanks," I said. "I should probably get back, in case they're ready to go."

"Okay," Shelly said. "Let's see if they've decided to take that pup home with them." She stared at me for a moment. Maybe my face looked as sad as I felt. "You all right?"

"I just wish . . . I wish things were different."

Wait. What did I just say?

Hadn't I wished for months that things would go back to the way they used to be? That Mom and Dad were happily married. That we still lived in Bakersfield. That Inca and I were inseparable, like always.

Did I still wish that? Sometimes, I guess. But I think I'd finally realized it was a wish that would never come true. And wishes should be possible, shouldn't they? Like, what's the point of wishing for a million dollars every single day when a million dollars isn't just going to fall from the sky?

As I thought about my friend and her family and what they were going through, I didn't want to spend my time wishing for things that were impossible. Not only that, I'd give up every single wish I'd ever had if it would help Carmen.

When Emma and I had thrown our bottles into the ocean, we'd wished that someone would respond. And the best possible thing had happened—we'd become friends with Carmen. And now just about all I wanted in the world was for her to feel safe and happy.

I *really* wanted to give Carmen and Oscar a cat to love. But I wanted to give them a lot more than that, too.

Shelly put her arm around me and gave me a squeeze. "I'm sorry, hon. I know it's difficult to leave them behind. Believe me, I'd take each and every one of them home if I could."

Back out in the meet-and-greet area, Emma and her

brother were still on the floor with the dog. When Emma saw me, she said, "Since Lance found him, he decided he should pick the name."

"Meet Captain Jack Sparrow," Lance said with a huge grin. "You know, from *Pirates of the Caribbean*? We'll call him Jack for short."

I smiled as I bent down to pet the adorable dog now named Jack. "So I guess that means he's yours?"

Emma hopped up and grabbed my hands as she jumped up and down. "We get a dog, we get a dog! I'm so happy." Then she turned around and gave her dad a big hug.

Before we could take him home, though, there was paperwork to fill out and lots of instructions about what they'd need to do and buy to make Jack comfortable in his new home.

"Can you go to the pet store with us?" Emma asked. "You can come home and have dinner with us afterward, if you want."

"Sure," I said. "I'll text my mom and let her know."

On the way, Jack sat between Emma and me in the back seat. Emma couldn't stop smiling. She was so lucky, I thought. If only Carmen could have a little bit of luck, too.

It doesn't seem fair that...

* *some people are born rich and other people are born poor.*
* *some people get everything they want and other people get very little.*
* *people with brown or black skin are looked at differently by some people.*
* *there are so many unwanted pets.*
* *kids go hungry in the richest country in the world.*
* *kids are afraid of violence at school and lots of adults don't seem to care.*
* *life is unfair. But it is. And I guess the sooner you just accept it, the better?*

Twenty-Two

THANKS, MOM

When I got home, Mom was on the couch, watching a movie. The house smelled good, like chocolate. Is there any better smell in the world? My dad would probably say a fresh-cut lawn. And to that I'd say, "Then you eat your lawn and I'll eat the chocolate."

"Did Miranda make something?" I asked Mom.

"Yes," Mom said as she leaned forward, grabbed the remote off the coffee table, and hit the pause button. "Brownies. You want some?"

"In a little while. Where is she, anyway?"

"In her room, doing homework." Mom patted the spot next to her. "Did you guys get everything they need for Jack?"

I dropped my backpack on the floor and plopped down on the couch. "Yep. Got him a dog bed and a crate and some toys. Oh, and food, obviously."

"I'm so happy for them," Mom said, smiling. "And Jack, too. Especially Jack."

"I think they're going to come see you at work," I said. "Make sure he has all his shots and stuff."

"Good," she said. "I can't wait to meet him."

"I looked at the cats while we were at the shelter," I told her. "I found one I think Carmen and Oscar would love."

"Oh, sweetie," Mom said as she put her arm around me.

"What if I help pay for it?" I asked, leaning into her. "Maybe I can raise the prices on my artwork. If I gave them a couple hundred dollars, would that feed him for a year?"

She turned a little so she was facing me. Then she put her hand on my leg and said, "Juliet, I know you really want to help them. And I love that you have such a big heart. But I've been thinking about it, and it's not just about the money. You really shouldn't go against their mother's wishes. Having a pet is like adding another member of the family, and she probably doesn't feel like she can take that on right now."

"But I want to *do* something," I said, my voice shaking. "Carmen is working hard to save the bookmobile, but what about her and her family? Who's going to save them, Mom?"

And when Mom's eyes filled with tears, I couldn't keep mine in anymore. We sat there and held each other and I cried. Because sometimes? Sometimes you just need to sit with your mom and cry.

After she got me the box of tissues and my sniffling had

gone from ridiculous to only slightly annoying, Mom sat next to me and lovingly tucked my hair behind my ears. "I know it hurts to see your friend hurting," she said. "And maybe you can't take that away completely, but you are helping her by being her friend. I want you to know that and believe it."

"What if I want to do more?" I asked.

"Then we need to think about that and see what we can come up with," Mom said. "If this is something you feel strongly about, maybe you need to share your feelings with people who make the laws."

"Could I write a letter to someone?" I asked.

"Absolutely," Mom said. "You could write to our state senator. You could also write to the editor of the newspaper. They print letters from concerned citizens once a week and that can be a very powerful thing, to have your opinion read by thousands of people."

"Except when we wrote letters to Mr. Strickland at the grocery store, they didn't do any good. I mean, he didn't change his mind or anything."

"Maybe not," Mom said, "but you know what? You tried. And that counts for something. If no one tries to change things, guess what happens?"

"Nothing?" I asked.

"That's exactly right," she said. "Absolutely nothing. Think about baseball players going up to bat. They strike out sometimes. That's part of the game. But one strikeout doesn't mean they should never try to hit a ball again. Because the next one? The next one could be a home run. You just never know."

"Wow," I said. "I never thought about it like that." I stood up. "Okay, I have a lot to do, then. On top of writing letters, I still have five more pieces I want to paint, and the arts and crafts fair is in four days."

"How are you doing on supplies?" Mom asked. "Anything I can get you?"

"You know, I'm worried about how I'm going to display everything," I told her. "Ms. Strickland said every booth will come with a table, but anything else you want, you have to bring yourself."

"Let me see if I can find some easels," Mom said. "I think that's what you need. You probably won't be able to display all the paintings at one time, but maybe you do six or seven and, when you sell one, you replace it with a new one." She looked around. "Where are you storing all the ones you've finished, anyway?"

"In my closet," I said. "Stacked on the floor."

"I'm proud of you, Juju Bean," she said. "You're doing a good thing. Many good things, actually."

"Thanks," I said as I headed to the kitchen to get a brownie and a glass of milk before I went to my room. I was already writing a letter in my head. I checked the time. It was just after seven. I had a little bit of homework to do and then I'd write a letter and paint a picture.

My phone buzzed in my pocket. I pulled it out as I munched on my brownie, and found a picture from Emma. It was Jack, sleeping in his new dog bed, a fuzzy yellow blanket wrapped around him so all that was sticking out was his head.

She wrote: A whole new world! (Imagine me singing the song from "Aladdin.")

I wrote back: A whole new world in a happy home with so many people to love him. Lucky dog!

She responded with a bunch of heart emojis and little doggy faces and footprints.

I sent her a photo of Casper I had taken last week and wrote: Tell Jack that Casper says hi and welcome to the neighborhood. He'd bake him some dog biscuits but he's worn himself out from sleeping all day.

She replied: Want me to bring him over sometime so they can become friends? Jack might love cats, you never know.

Yes, or he might love to eat them, Emma. Not really sure I want to find out which one it is.

This time she responded with a row of cat and dog emojis and said: Think positively, Juliet! Maybe they'd become the best of friends and we could create a YouTube channel about Jack and Casper and everyone would tune in to see the cutest dog and the cutest cat being adorable together. We could make millions!

How does Emma even do that? I want a brain like that.

Dear Editor,

I think it's sad that some people in our community are scared of being deported. They have families and they're working hard to give them the best life they can. If they aren't doing anything wrong, why should they be sent away?

I know a kid who is scared every day that her mother is going to be sent back to Guatemala, leaving her and her little brother all alone. I asked her why her parents came to America and she said they wanted to escape the horrible gang violence that was happening in their country. They just wanted to make a better life for themselves.

My friend loves helping other people. I look up to her so much. She's the kind of person who makes America a better place. Maybe people who are scared of immigrants need to actually get to know some of them. They're just regular people who love their families and want to be happy. That's all.

Signed,
Juliet Kelley
San Diego, CA

Twenty-Three

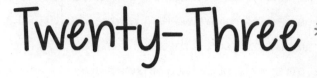

THE BIG DAY

Somehow, I did it. I finished the paintings. Every time my brain tried to tell me there was no point to any of it, I told it to be quiet and go sit in the corner because I had decided I was going to do it. And then I would paint a picture and pretend it was for my friends, who seemed to love everything I made.

Brains like to play tricks on us, I think. So maybe the best thing is to play a trick right back. If my brain thought I was painting a picture for someone who would love it no matter what, it was a lot easier to get it done.

Still, when I woke up the day of the arts and crafts fair and thought about walking into the senior center with my artwork, it felt like someone had twisted my intestines into a pretzel.

My twenty-five paintings were boxed up and ready to go. Mom had found a bright blue tablecloth along with some little easels online and had ordered them for me. I'd made a sign that said each painting cost fifteen dollars. I had planned on asking for ten, but Miranda said I could easily ask for more. Since I wanted to raise as much money as possible to help the Buttons, I'd decided to increase the price. It seemed like there wasn't anything else to do. I was ready. Except I didn't *feel* ready. I felt nervous and afraid.

I remembered what Miranda had said. I needed to talk to myself like I'd talk to a friend.

You can do this, Juliet. People will love your paintings. And for every one you sell, you are helping your friends, Mr. and Mrs. Button. That's the important thing.

You can do this.

You can do this.

You can do this.

Then I crossed my fingers, closed my eyes, and silently made a wish. *Please, let people love my work. Let me sell my paintings and make lots of money for the bookmobile.*

There was a knock at my door. I sat up. "Come in."

"Juliet," Mom said, waving a newspaper around, "they ran your letter in the paper this morning!"

"No way," I said.

Mom put the folded paper in front of me, so I picked it up and started reading. Mine was one of four letters they'd printed, and they'd put mine first. "Wow" was all I could manage.

"It's really good," Mom said. "So proud of you. Now get

up and hop in the shower. It's your big day and we want to make sure you have lots of time to get your table ready."

You can do this, I told myself again.

But what if I really couldn't?

I decided to take a bath instead of a shower. I thought it might help me relax. I stayed in the tub so long, I wondered if I might magically turn into a mermaid. As I dreamt of swimming in the ocean with my sparkly mermaid tail splashing behind me, Miranda knocked on the door and yelled, "Juliet, are you okay in there?"

I reluctantly got out, threw the towel around me, and opened the door.

"I don't know if I can do this," I told her. So much for the positive self-talk.

"Juliet, stop with the drama," she said. "It's going to be fine. Please, just get dressed. Mom's making omelets and then you need to go."

As she walked away, I called out, "I'll remember your extremely helpful pep talk next weekend when you have your lifeguard tryouts!"

After I put on a gray skirt with a yellow-and-gray floral shirt, I checked my phone and found I had a text from Emma. All she said was "The big day is here!" with a bunch of clapping emojis. Well, at least someone was excited.

I ate a few bites of my omelet, but that's all I could manage. After we finished, Mom and I packed up the car and headed out.

"It's so nice that the senior center is donating the space for this," Mom said. "How are you girls collecting donations for the bookmobile?"

"Emma's in charge of that," I said, looking out the window. "I think her mom was going to help draft a little note to everyone about the bookmobile and then at the end of the day, they'll go around with a box and collect donations."

"Hm. I wonder if you should have made the donation mandatory in order for people to participate in the fair," Mom said. "I worry . . ."

Her voice trailed off. "What?" I asked.

She reached over and patted my leg, smiling as she did. "Never mind. I'm sure it'll be fine. People love to help other people, right? Yes. It'll be fine."

"I hope so," I said. "Otherwise all this will have been for nothing. Oh, Mom, I just remembered I wanted to ask—did Dad tell you he's coming?"

"Yes, he did."

"Are you okay with it?"

"Absolutely. I'm happy he wants to support you. That's what parents are supposed to do."

"It won't be, like, awkward for you?"

"I don't think so. But even if it is, that shouldn't be your concern, Juliet. We're adults and we'll handle it. My main priority, and your dad's, too, is that you and Miranda feel loved and supported. And I think both of us are committed to doing whatever is required to make that happen. I think he's going to come for Miranda's lifeguard tryouts next week as well."

I wondered if she felt bad that he had to drive so far to see us. But I decided not to ask. It wouldn't do any good, and anyway, I did like it here. More than I'd thought I would.

When we got to the senior center, Mom dropped me off at the door and then went to look for a place to park. I carried the box with the tablecloth and easels so I could start getting my spot ready. There were signs pointing the way to the recreation room, where the fair was being held. A smiling Emma holding a stack of papers greeted me when I reached the large set of double doors to the rec room.

"You're here!" she said. She stood up straight and smiled as she said, "Thank you for being a part of our arts and crafts fair. We're doing this to raise money to save the bookmobile, and a donation in any amount is appreciated. I'll be coming by later with a donation box. In the meantime, I hope you have a wonderful and successful day. Would you like a flyer that tells you more about the bookmobile and why we believe it's an important part of our community that deserves to stay?"

I laughed. "No, I'm good, thanks. And wow, you've got that down. Nice."

"Thanks," she said, her cheeks turning a little pink. "I've been practicing a lot. Hey, Carmen's already in there. Your table is a few down from hers."

"I'm so glad she decided to sell her mom's jewelry," I said.

"Me, too," Emma said. "You are both doing a big, scary thing, and I'm so proud of you."

"If I don't sell anything, promise not to laugh at me?" I asked her.

Her mouth dropped open. "You know I'd never do that. And you're going to sell them. I promise you, I'm right about this."

I took a deep breath. "Well, I guess we're about to find out."

I started to walk in when Emma called back, "Oh! I almost forgot. I saw your letter to the editor this morning in the paper. It's so cool you did that."

I gave her a puzzled look. "You read the paper?"

"No, but Lance does and he saw it and told me about it."

"I was so upset I couldn't get Carmen and Oscar a cat," I explained. "My mom said I should I do some other things that might help get the laws changed or whatever."

"Yeah, I get it. I brought the paper in for Carmen to read. I bet it'll mean a lot to her to see how much you want to help her."

Just then my mom walked up carrying one of the boxes with my paintings in it. She smiled at Emma and told her good morning before she said to me, "You're not stalling, are you, honey? Let's get in there and get this party started."

"Okay, okay," I said.

We found our table and Mom immediately got to work spreading the blue tablecloth out and setting up the easels. I went over to Carmen's table, where she had necklaces and bracelets laid out. She'd made a handmade sign, just like I had, with the prices. A bracelet was four dollars and a necklace cost seven.

I picked one up and couldn't believe how much it looked like real beads. "These are so beautiful," I told her.

"Thanks," she muttered.

I set the jewelry down and looked at her. "Carmen? Is everything okay?"

She shook her head and stared at me. "Why'd you do that, Juliet?"

"Do what?"

"Why'd you write that letter?"

"I was . . . I was trying to help. I wanted people to know—"

"Juliet," Mom called. "I need you to come and choose the paintings you want to display first, please."

But I didn't want to go. Was Carmen mad? Worried? Both? What was it—what was going on?

"Juliet?" Mom said again.

"Coming," I said.

Instead of dipping my toes into a puddle of worry, it now felt like I'd just jumped into a giant pit of anxiety.

Things I try when I'm feeling anxious

* *Deep breaths*
* *Painting*
* *Reading a good book*
* *More deep breaths*
* *Soft music*
* *Going for a walk*
* *Taking a nap*
* *Baking something with my sister*

(Sitting in a big room with people walking by, judging my art? Not so much.)

Twenty-Four

ARTIST IN PAIN

Looking around my table, I could see some of the other things being sold. Knitted items like baby blankets and hats. Some pottery. Homemade soap. Candles. Jewelry. Photography. And art, though mine was a lot simpler than the others. I didn't know if that was a good thing or a bad thing.

When the doors opened, a wave of people streamed in. I don't know why it surprised me, but it did. Ms. Strickland had obviously done a really good job getting the word out.

A girl I recognized from school walked up to my table with her mom. "Oh wow, I love your owls," the girl said.

"Thanks," I said. "I love your hijab. It's beautiful." It was a gorgeous emerald green.

"Thank you," she said as she stared at an owl I'd painted teal and purple.

"We go to the same school," I told her. "I'm pretty new, so you probably don't recognize me. My name's Juliet."

She smiled. "I'm Nayah." When she pulled a twenty-dollar bill out of her pants pocket, I thought I might cry. "I'd like to buy this one, please. I know exactly where I'm going to put it in my room."

I took her money and gave her change from a cash box I'd brought with me, and then I wrapped the painting for her.

"Thank you," she said as I handed it to her. "I really love it."

Hearing her say that was the best feeling. And it showed that my brain had been lying to me about no one wanting my stuff. Thank goodness I had figured out how to turn the negative voices off.

"Good," I said. "I'm glad." More than glad, really. Ecstatic.

As she left, more people walked up, including my dad. He came around to my side of the table and gave me a quick hug. "I'll be back when things slow down a bit," he told me. "Your paintings are incredible, Juliet. Really."

"Thanks for coming," I said. "Hey, can you go buy something from my friend Carmen?" I pointed in the direction of her table. "She's the one selling the beaded necklaces."

"Sure," he said. "Should I pick something out for you and your sister?"

"I'd love that, thanks!"

An elderly lady bought one of my cat paintings because

it reminded her of one she'd had as a child. And I sold two night sky pictures to a pregnant woman who told me she planned on hanging them in the nursery.

My nervousness about selling my work faded fast, but worry didn't disappear completely because I couldn't stop thinking about Carmen. I hadn't mentioned her name in my letter to the editor, so I thought she'd be okay with it. I never would have written the letter if I'd known it would upset her. And maybe that's why she was mad. I probably should have asked her if she'd mind.

Once it slowed down, I took a quick break to text Emma, telling her Carmen was upset with me and I didn't know what to do. Before I finished, I heard, "Hello, Juliet." I looked up and saw Mrs. Button.

I got up from my chair. "Hi! How are you?"

"I'm doing well, thank you. And I'm so tickled you girls are putting this fair on to help us." Her eyes got teary. "It really means the world to us. Truly. Thank you."

"I just hope we raise enough to pay the rent for a year," I told her.

"Every little bit will help," she said. "So don't worry at all." She looked down and picked up one of my tree pictures, one sprinkled with pink cherries among the leaves. "You are so talented, Juliet. I don't know how people choose. I love them all."

I felt my cheeks get warm. "Thank you. They're kind of simple, but—"

"Oh, no. There's nothing simple about creating a piece of art that makes someone's heart feel like it's wrapped in a soft, warm blanket. Cozy. Comforted. Happy."

"It makes you feel like that?" I asked.

"Yes," she said. "It does. You have a gift, and I'm so glad you're sharing it with others today."

A woman and her young daughter stepped up just then to look at the paintings. "I'm going to wander around and look at all the wonderful creations," Mrs. Button said, giving me a wink as she did.

"Okay. Carmen's table is that way," I said, gesturing in the right direction. "Make sure to look at the pretty jewelry her mom made with her help. It's amazing."

"I certainly will," Mrs. Button said.

Dad came back a few minutes later carrying a few bags. "You've been busy," I said.

"There's a lot of good stuff here," he said, smiling. "And I'm not done." He picked up two paintings, one a simple purple gerbera daisy in a vase and the other a picture of Casper.

"Who are those for?" I asked.

"I miss Casper, so that one is for me. And the other one you can give to Inca the next time you come to stay."

"Thanks, Dad," I said.

"You're welcome."

For the next few hours, I was pretty busy. Dad sat with me for some of the time and helped talk to people because that was the part that got kind of tiring. People loved asking me questions, like how long have I been painting, how did I choose what to paint, and on and on. The good news? I sold twenty-four of my twenty-five paintings. When it was time to clean up, Emma came around with a box for donations. Her jaw dropped as she watched me put half of the cash I'd collected into the box. "That's a lot of money. Are you sure?"

"That's why we're here, isn't it?" I said.

"Wow," she said. "You're awesome."

Now if only I could convince Carmen to think the same thing of me. Dad had left to go see a friend and Mom was talking to Emma's mom, so it seemed like a good time. I took a deep breath and walked over to Carmen's table. I didn't know what to say, though.

"It looked like you were really busy," I said. I didn't want to ask her if she sold a lot, because if she didn't, she might feel bad. But I hoped she had.

"Yeah," she said. "Sold almost everything."

"Carmen, way to go!" She wasn't looking at me, though. She was focusing on putting the last few things in the big beach bag she had brought.

"I'm so sorry," I said. "For writing that letter and not asking you if it was okay with you. I should have asked and I just . . . I didn't even think about it."

Now she looked at me, and it was like a dark shadow of sadness covered her eyes. "What if they want to know who it is that you wrote about?"

It surprised me that she'd have to even ask. "I'd never tell them, Carmen. Never."

"But what if they have ways of finding out?"

She was afraid. Because of me, she was even more afraid than she'd been before. I couldn't believe I'd done that to her. I didn't know what to say. What to do. I wanted to make it all go away. But I couldn't take the letter back. I couldn't do anything. Somehow I managed to say "I'm sorry" once more before I ran back to my table, grabbed the boxes, and ran out of the room.

"Juliet?" Mom called out.

I turned around, trying hard to keep myself from bursting into tears right there, in front of everyone. "Can I wait for you at the car?" I asked.

"Sure," she said. "I'll be right there."

I glanced at Carmen before I left. My friend who loved Vincent van Gogh as much as I did. Who loved ice cream and hated sharks. My friend who wanted to make a secret club to help make people's wishes come true. My sweet, sweet friend.

At least, I hoped she was still my friend.

Dear Carmen,

I'm sorry.

I can't say it enough. I'm so sorry.

When I went to the shelter with Emma to get Captain Jack Sparrow, I found a gray kitty that I wanted to get you and your brother. But I couldn't go against your mom's wishes. So I had to think of something else I could do to try and help you.

I should have asked you first. But I didn't and now all I can do is apologize and hope you forgive me.

Love,

Your friend, Juliet

Starry Beach Club Member #2

Twenty-Five

SURPRISE!

We spent Mother's Day doing all the things my mom wanted to do. We went out for brunch, bought some fresh flowers, and finally went shopping for artwork for our empty walls. The whole time, I thought about Carmen and her mom. I hoped they were having a good day together and that I hadn't ruined it for them.

As we worked together to hang the prints in the family room, Mom said, "Juliet, I'm proud of you. I know you were scared about selling your art yesterday, but you did it."

Miranda reached over for a high five. "You go, girl. Sold almost all of them!"

I slapped her hand and then said, "Yeah. I didn't let the invisible sharks stop me."

She looked very confused. "I know we're close to the water, but we're not *that* close."

"Sorry," I said with a smile. "Long story."

Mom chimed in as she marked the wall with her pencil so we knew where to hang the next print. "If you mean you shouldn't worry until you see a shark actually coming at you, I agree with you a hundred percent. That's what mindfulness teaches you, something I've been trying to practice more of, by doing meditation. We need to do our best to live in the moment and not worry about what may or may not come in the future."

"Mother," Miranda said, "you're not going to run off and join the monks, are you?"

Mom laughed. "Only if you keep calling me Mother!"

Monday, when I got to school, I slipped the card I'd made for Carmen with my apology note into her locker. On the front of the card, I'd drawn a picture of three girls holding hands as they stood on the beach looking out at the ocean. As I'd drawn it, I'd thought about what my new life in San Diego would have been like if I hadn't met Emma and then Carmen. Would I have tried to become friends with Apple, the first girl I probably would have met at school, even if she didn't seem like the type I'd usually hang out with? Or maybe I would have wandered around, friendless for days, missing everyone and everything back in Bakersfield. It was hard to know, and the good thing was, I didn't have to. Emma and Carmen had welcomed me with open arms and loving hearts. I'd been so lucky. And now it felt like my luck had been thrown into the ocean and was sinking like a gigantic anchor.

After I got my stuff from my locker, I headed to blue hall to find Emma. And maybe Carmen, if she'd talk to me. But when I turned the corner and saw both of them talking and laughing, I stopped midstep and did an about-face. I couldn't do it. I couldn't interrupt them. Emma was good at making people laugh while all I seemed to be good at was making people miserable. Carmen deserved to be happy for a few minutes without me ruining it.

The morning dragged on, and when lunchtime came around, I wasn't sure what to do. But once again, Emma came to my rescue.

"We're not eating in the cafeteria today," she said. I stared at her, with her cute pink pants and gray-and-white striped shirt.

"Where are we going?"

She smiled. "You'll see. Follow me."

We went down the hall and out to a courtyard with four picnic tables. I hadn't even known they were there. Outside, it was warm and sunny. Three of the tables were full with kids talking and laughing, but one of them had just one person—Carmen.

I sat down across from her. "Hi," I said.

"Hi," she replied softly, avoiding eye contact.

"I have a bunch of surprises for you guys," Emma said as

she set a big brown bag in front of us. "The first one being that I made us peanut butter and pickle sandwiches for lunch. Have you ever had one, Juliet?"

I tried to imagine what that might taste like and I couldn't do it. "Nope."

"They're really good. But in case you don't like them, I also brought a PB&J." She started singing, *"Peanut, peanut butter, jam."* She made jazzy hands when she sang *jam* and I couldn't help but smile. "Or maybe, peanut, peanut butter, pickle!"

"I'm afraid to try the peanut butter and pickle one," Carmen said.

"Me, too," I said. "I love pickles, you know that. But . . ."

"Okay, hold on," Emma said as she went to work pulling sandwiches, a bag of chips, three small water bottles, and napkins out of the bag. "We'll get back to the sandwiches in a minute, then. I have more surprises, but not until we 'talk it out.'" When she said "talk it out," she put her hands up and made air quotes. "That's what my dad says when a fight goes on for days at our house and everyone's sick of it," she explained.

This was my cue. I took a deep breath and said, "Like I said in the card I made for you, I'm really sorry, Carmen. I was just trying to help. I wanted to do something."

Carmen fiddled with her napkin. She didn't say anything for a long time. Finally, she said, "I know, but . . . what if someone finds out the person you were talking about is me?"

Now she looked up, tears pooling in her eyes. "They could come for my mom. And this isn't something one letter can fix, you know?"

"I don't think anyone will find out," I said. "I promise, I'd never tell them. And maybe it can't fix things, but maybe . . . maybe people will see that real people are hurting and it's wrong and things need to change."

Emma sat down next to me and reached her hands across the table toward our friend. "Carmen? We love you. We don't want anything to happen to you."

Carmen nodded. "I know your heart was in the right place, Juliet. It's just . . ." She started to cry. "I'm so worried for my mom."

While she wiped at her face with the napkin, Emma went around to her side of the table, sat down, and pulled our friend into her arms.

I thought about what my mom had said. About the invisible sharks and how it's too easy to live your life like they're coming for you. Like, we make up stories in our mind and, pretty soon, they seem so real, we believe them. I'd done more reading about the immigrant situation, and fear seemed to be the main reason some people didn't want them here. That fear created fear in people like Carmen, and then all you ended up with was a whole bunch of people afraid. Of course, Carmen had every right to be afraid. But sitting around, thinking about it all the time? That didn't seem very good.

"Maybe until the sharks are in plain sight, we shouldn't be so scared," I said.

Carmen gave me a funny look, kind of like my sister had yesterday. "I don't know what you mean."

Before I could try to explain, Emma jumped in. "My mom always says worrying is like sitting in a rocking chair. You worry and worry, and it doesn't get you anywhere. And all you get is more gray hairs. Well, when you're my mom's age, anyway."

"That's one of the reasons why I wanted to start the club," Carmen said. "To keep myself from being so scared and worried all the time."

"I know!" Emma said. "And now is a perfect time to talk about surprise number two. You guys, we raised a little over four hundred dollars from the arts and crafts fair. That's a lot, right? I bet it's enough to save the bookmobile. Want to go with me after school to give the Buttons the money?"

"Yes!" we both said, a little bit too loudly, because some of the kids at the other tables gave us funny looks.

"And now, surprise number three," Emma said as she got up, went to her backpack, pulled out a newspaper, and tossed it on the table. "Three more people have written letters to the editor, agreeing with Juliet, talking about how wrong it is that people in our community are scared and that we need to do something."

"Really?" I asked, picking up the paper. She'd circled the letters with a red pen so they'd be easy to find. As I

read, I realized Carmen should hear what others were saying. She should know there were people standing up for her.

"'Dear Editor,'" I read. "'I agree with Juliet. Immigrants are regular people who are only trying to make a good life for themselves and their families. And kids like Juliet's friend shouldn't be afraid of being left without parents. What kind of country are we that would do that to children?'"

"Here's another one," I said. "'Dear Editor: Diversity doesn't make our community or our country weaker. It makes us stronger. I am a businessman who has had many Latinos work for me and I'm here to tell you they are some of the most hardworking people I've ever met. Not only that but I find they are deeply committed to their families and have kind and generous hearts. I want kids like Juliet to know I support immigrants 100 percent and I know there are many others like me.'"

"I think there are a lot of people who don't like what's happening," Emma said. "And last night at dinner, my family was discussing it and I got an idea, which is surprise number four. I want to start a Social Action Club here at school."

"What's that?" I asked.

"Yeah, I don't know, either," Carmen said.

"It's a club where we find changes we want to make in the world and then we come up with projects and activities to do."

"It sounds like trying to make wishes come true in a bigger way," I said, excited at the thought.

"A much bigger way," Carmen said.

"Exactly," Emma said. "What do you think? If we can find a teacher to help us, we can get the club started and then invite others to join us. And maybe immigration is the first thing on our list."

"I'm in," I said.

"Me, too," Carmen said.

"Good," Emma said. "Now, pick up those sandwiches I made and try them. Please?"

"Are they dill or sweet pickles?" I asked.

"Dill," Emma said. "I've tried it with both and I think dill is better."

I put the sandwich to my lips and took a bite. And it was . . . good!

"Wow!" I said. "I can't believe it."

"Carmen?" Emma asked as Carmen took a bite as well. "What do you think?"

"How is that even possible?" Carmen asked. "I thought it'd be so gross."

"Just like Juliet thought she wouldn't sell a single painting?" Emma asked. Then she broke into song. *"Everything is possible."*

I knew that song. Shawn Mendes. But it was hard to sing with a mouthful of peanut butter and pickles, so I happily left the singing to Emma.

Ideas for the Social Action Club

* *Plant trees to help the environment*
* *Do a "no straw" challenge at school to keep them from going into landfills*
* *Have a canned food drive to help feed hungry people in our neighborhood*
* *Plant a community garden and let kids take food home if they need it*
* *Write postcards to senators to try and get laws changed*
* *Make yard signs that say, "Choose Love, Not Hate"*
* *Have the arts and crafts fair every year and donate money to a different cause each time*

Twenty-Six

WE DO

"We have a surprise for you," Emma sang out as we stepped into the bookmobile, which smelled like books and Mrs. Button's floral perfume.

"Oh, goody," Mr. Button said as he put his book into his lap. "I love surprises."

"Hello, girls," Mrs. Button said. "So nice to see you today."

Mr. Button was sitting in his usual chair next to the front counter. Mrs. Button was sitting behind the counter, once again writing in her notebook of beautiful things. I thought back to when she'd given me and Emma notebooks of our own. It was such a nice thing to do. These were two of the nicest people I'd ever met, and it felt so good to be giving something to them as a way to say thank you.

"I've been thinking a lot about generosity today," Mrs. Button told us. "About how even a small act can have such an enormous impact. When you drop a pebble in a lake, it's hard to count the ripples it creates. I think the same might be true of generosity."

"Totally," Carmen said. "When someone does something nice for me, it makes me want to do something nice for someone else, you know?"

"Yes!" Emma said. "It's contagious. But a lot more fun than catching a cold."

"Isn't that the truth?" Mr. Button said with a chuckle.

Emma took her backpack off and dug into the side pocket. She pulled out an envelope with the words *For Mr. and Mrs. Button* written on the outside.

"We're so happy to be able to give you this," Emma said, holding the envelope out for Mrs. Button. "We raised a bunch of money, and hopefully it's enough to save the bookmobile."

"Well, I'll be," Mr. Button said.

"Oh my goodness," Mrs. Button said as she got to her feet. "You really managed to raise a thousand dollars? What an incredible accomplishment."

She took the envelope from Emma's hands and as she did, it felt like the earth was dropping out from under me. A thousand dollars? We'd never actually asked how much they needed, and now I realized, we should have.

"Um," Emma said. "I . . . we thought four hundred would probably be enough. Like, it seems like so much. But you need more than double that?"

The smiles disappeared from their faces. "I'm afraid so," Mrs. Button said.

Mr. Button jumped in, trying to make us feel better. "Four hundred dollars puts a big dent in it, so don't you girls feel bad at all."

"It's wonderful, what you've done," Mrs. Button told us. "You should be very proud of yourselves."

"It's not enough, though," I said. "But you know what? I have some more money at home." I turned to leave. "I'll go get it for you."

"No, no, please," Mrs. Button said. "You don't need to do that. We'll figure this out, girls. Please don't worry yourselves about it."

There was that word again. Too many worries and not enough happy things, like squirrel monkeys and sunsets and ice cream cones. We'd wanted to fix something. To make life better for someone. Or in this case, a lot of someones—people who used the bookmobile. And coming close didn't really count, did it?

When the door opened behind us, we all turned to see who it was. What a surprise when Mr. Dooney and Ms. Strickland walked in. Carmen, Emma, and I stepped out of the way to make more room.

"Are you having a party?" Mr. Dooney asked. "If so, you forgot to invite us."

"We'd never have a party without you, Fred,"

Mrs. Button said. "The girls were just dropping off the money they made from the arts and crafts fair."

"Oh, then this is perfect timing," Ms. Strickland said. "I've come to give you this private donation someone left." She turned to us. "After you'd gone home on Saturday, I found this envelope at my desk. It's a five-hundred-dollar donation. Isn't that wonderful?"

While Emma, Carmen, and I tried to get over the shock of what had just happened, Mr. Button reached into his wallet and pulled out five twenty-dollar bills. "I was going to buy myself a fancy new blender, but I suppose the old one works just fine for now."

"Oh my gosh," I said as I grabbed my friends' hands and started jumping up and down. "There's enough. That makes a thousand dollars. The bookmobile can stay!"

We squealed and jumped around and hugged one another. When we felt the bookmobile shake, we burst out laughing.

After we settled down, Mr. Dooney said, "Say, while we have you girls here, we'd like to ask you something. Since you three are so good at coordinating events, we wondered if you might like to help with another one."

"Probably depends on what it is," Emma said. "Like, if you want us to put together a shark-viewing party, that's not really our thing."

Carmen and I laughed.

"No sharks involved," Ms. Strickland said. "Just flowers, a minister, and some of our closest friends."

No way. Was this really happening?

"You're getting married?" Emma blurted out. "The two of you?"

They laughed. "You sound surprised," Ms. Strickland asked. "Perhaps because we're not exactly spring chickens anymore?"

"You just . . . you haven't known each other that long," I said.

"When you get to be our age," Mr. Dooney said, "you realize life is short and time is precious. We've enjoyed each other's company so much, and we've both been alone for a while now, and, well . . . we don't want to be alone any longer."

Ms. Strickland chimed in. "Our hearts tell us it's the right thing to do, and so, we're going to take the leap."

"It seems to me there's been a lot of leaping lately," Mrs. Button said as she gave me a wink. "Why, look what a leap into an arts and crafts fair has done for us."

"Yes," Mr. Button said. "I do believe that it often takes a leap for people to see that they can really soar."

That was definitely one for the notebook of beautiful things.

"So what do you girls say?" Mr. Dooney asked. "Can we count on you to help? We'll give you a budget and set you loose, how does that sound?"

The Starry Beach Club would join forces again. We'd create a magical wedding and reception for a wonderful couple.

"We do," Emma said. She turned to me. "Get it? Instead of I do, we do?"

"You're so clever," I said, laughing.

"Wait, when is it?" Emma asked, turning back to Mr. Dooney and Ms. Strickland.

"We thought the end of June would be a fine time for a wedding," Ms. Strickland said. "We'll have a simple ceremony on the beach. It's the reception afterward that we really need help with. Nothing too fancy, though. Do you think a little over a month is enough time? We thought we'd use the rec room at the senior center, so the venue is taken care of."

"No problem," Emma said with all the confidence in the world. "But would it be okay with you if we had a bunch of different pies instead of cake? Something different, you know?"

"Oh, I love that idea," Ms. Strickland said. "Perhaps we can tell guests that instead of bringing a gift to the reception, they can bring a pie to share."

"A pie party," I said. "We get to have a pie party!"

This was going to be the best wedding ever. Hopefully.

Things needed for a wedding reception

* *A band or a DJ for dancing*
* *Coffee, tea, and punch to go with the pie*
* *Ice cream, maybe? Because apple pie without ice cream is sad.*
* *Centerpieces and tablecloths*
* *Flowers*
* *A guest book*
* *Plates, napkins, silverware, and glasses*
* *Decorations*

Twenty-Seven

SPLENDID

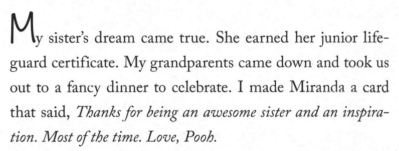

My sister's dream came true. She earned her junior life-guard certificate. My grandparents came down and took us out to a fancy dinner to celebrate. I made Miranda a card that said, *Thanks for being an awesome sister and an inspiration. Most of the time. Love, Pooh.*

When we went to visit Dad two weeks before the wedding, he was understanding when I spent a lot of time on his laptop looking at centerpiece ideas. Emma, Carmen, and I had already looked at so many, but nothing had seemed quite right.

Ms. Strickland said her favorite kind of flowers were tulips. We could have just gotten a bunch, split them up into vases, and called it good, but we wanted to do something unique. Maybe even extraordinary.

As I was shutting the computer down for the night, Dad said, "Girls? I need to tell you something."

He sounded nervous. Miranda shut off the television and we sat there, staring at him.

"I want you to be the first ones to know, I've met someone. Someone really special. And I'd love for you to meet her tomorrow. Thought we'd go out for lunch together, if that's all right?"

"You're not getting married, are you?" I asked.

"What?" He looked at me like I'd just asked if the sky was green. "No. No, honey, it's nothing like that. We're just dating. But it's important that you meet her and get to know her a little bit."

"Sorry," I said. "I have marriage on the brain, I guess, after all this stuff I've been doing for Mr. Dooney's wedding."

"That's understandable," he said.

"Who is it?" Miranda asked. "I mean, what's her name?"

"It's Andrea," he said. "From work. We've been friends for a while and it just kind of . . . blossomed into something more recently."

I could hardly stand the thought of Dad being with someone else. Miranda had told me to get used to the idea, because neither of our parents would want to stay single forever. But it wasn't easy to do. I didn't really want to let anyone else into our family. And that's what would have to happen when one of them got serious with someone one day.

One day, *down the road*, I told myself. *A long way down the road.*

Maybe the idea would get easier with time.

"Anyway," he continued, "I hope you like her."

Even though I had a lot of feelings about the whole thing, I really hoped so, too.

Sunday morning, Inca and I had a do-over doughnut date. When I walked in, she was sitting at our regular booth, waiting for me.

"Hi," I said, feeling a little shy, which was ridiculous. This was my best friend. But the last time we'd been here, things hadn't gone well. And I wanted this time to be different.

"Hey," she said.

I set a gift bag in front of her.

"What's this?" she asked.

"Open it and find out," I told her.

So she did. And when she saw the picture of the purple flower in a vase with my signature in the corner, she said, "Oh my gosh, I love it."

"It's from the arts and crafts fair I did. I feel like I should tell you that it was my dad's idea to get it for you. Maybe he was worried I wouldn't sell them all, I don't know. But anyway, happy June. Happy summer. Happy everything!"

She laughed. "You'll be here for part of the summer, right?"

"Yep. I guess Miranda isn't going to be able to come because of her new job. So it'll just be Dad and me for a few weeks. And maybe his girlfriend now and then."

Her eyes got big. "He has a girlfriend?"

"Yeah. We're meeting her later today."

"Wow," she said. "So much has changed."

I sighed. "Yeah."

"But we'll still go to the library a lot this summer when you're here, right?" she asked.

"For sure."

"And we'll still go swimming, right?"

"Yep."

"And we'll eat all the doughnuts we can stand, okay? Because no matter what happens, our love for doughnuts is forever."

Now I laughed. "Yes. And I can't wait."

She slid out of the booth. "You don't have to wait. Come on. I'm hungry."

Something told me it was going to be a really good summer.

A few hours later, I was sitting across the table from Andrea, in a little Italian restaurant eating salad and pasta and probably the best bread I'd ever had in my life. My stomach was having a very, very good day.

Andrea seemed pretty cool. She wore long, dangly earrings and had short silver hair with purple highlights. I loved it.

"Andrea oversees the education office at the zoo," Dad told us as we passed the bread basket around for the second time. "Like, she makes sure all the field trips go off without a hitch."

"Is it a hard job?" I asked.

"Only on the days when a child gets eaten by a big cat," she said. It made us all laugh.

"But in all seriousness," Dad said, "it's an important job. Making sure schoolchildren are safe and cared for while they're visiting."

Safe. Cared for. It made me think of Carmen and how it was all she wanted—for her and her family to be safe. If only she had someone working hard to protect her.

"I'm lucky," Andrea said. "It's a wonderful place to work. Any ideas as to what you want to do someday, girls? Or is it too soon, still?"

"Wedding planner, maybe, Juliet?" Dad asked.

"Should probably wait and see how it turns out first," Miranda joked.

"Thanks a lot," I told her. "It's hard to know, but sometimes I think I might like to write and illustrate books, maybe."

"She's very talented," Dad told Andrea.

"I want to travel," Miranda said. "See the world."

"Flight attendant could be fun," Dad said.

"I'm thinking pilot," Miranda said.

I felt proud of my fearless sister right then.

Dad's cheeks turned a little pink. Like he was embarrassed he hadn't thought of that. He took a drink of water before he said, "Absolutely. You girls are so smart. Whatever you decide to do, I'm sure you'll go far. Now, how about some dessert?"

"The spumoni ice cream is amazing," Andrea said. "If you like ice cream, of course."

"Love it," I said.

Andrea smiled. "Then I think we'll get along splendidly."

Later that afternoon, on the bus ride home, while Miranda slept, I thought about how sometimes people or things or situations didn't turn out exactly how I wanted them to be. My paintings were never as good as I'd like. The people Mom and Dad dated would probably never seem good enough, even if I liked them just fine. I'd never be able to do enough to help the people I cared about. But nothing, and nobody, is perfect. And if you wait around for things to be perfect, to feel perfect, or you try to be perfect yourself, you're going to miss out on so much.

My sister loved trying new recipes. Like the "Best Chocolate Cake (Ever)" recipe that turned out to really be the best chocolate cake ever. Seriously, it was so good. I probably would have looked at the recipe and decided it seemed too hard and skipped right over it. But she wasn't afraid to try. Or to leap, as Mr. Dooney had said.

I opened my notebook of beautiful things and wrote, *It can be scary to leap. It can feel like someone is pushing you off the edge of a cliff. But maybe those are the times when good things happen. When you realize you can do more than you ever imagined you could. When you discover you can soar.*

How to leap

1. *Tell yourself you are smart and strong and amazing.*
2. *Ignore anyone who tells you something else.*
3. *Focus on the positive things that can happen.*
4. *Find people who believe in you.*
5. *Make a chocolate cake and get a pep talk while you're at it.*
6. *Cross your fingers.*
7. *Make a wish that it will all turn out okay.*
8. *Do your best.*
9. *Show up.*
10. *Leap.*

Twenty-Eight

A FAVORITE NEW SONG

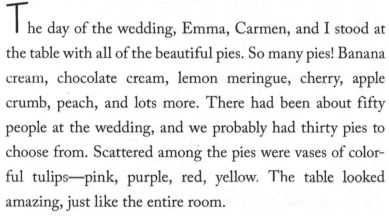

The day of the wedding, Emma, Carmen, and I stood at the table with all of the beautiful pies. So many pies! Banana cream, chocolate cream, lemon meringue, cherry, apple crumb, peach, and lots more. There had been about fifty people at the wedding, and we probably had thirty pies to choose from. Scattered among the pies were vases of colorful tulips—pink, purple, red, yellow. The table looked amazing, just like the entire room.

Emma's dad had found a handyman to string white Christmas lights across the ceiling in rows. Not only that, we'd bought ten large round paper lanterns and he'd hung those from the ceiling, too. Every table had white linen tablecloths with the pretty centerpieces we'd created. Mr. and Mrs. Dooney absolutely loved how it had turned out.

As I went back to staring at the pies, I said, "I wish I could have a slice of each one."

"I know," Emma said. "It's so hard to choose."

"Hello, girls," said a man's voice. I spun around and there was Mr. Strickland.

I stood there, not sure what to say. We'd seen him at the wedding and managed to avoid him. But now we were supposed to talk to the man who had told us to stop pestering him?

Emma managed to find her voice. "Hello, Mr. Strickland. Would you like a piece of pie?"

"Yes, I would, but I can get it myself," he replied. "I wanted to tell you, congratulations. I'm sure you're pleased the bookmobile is staying."

"Yes, we are," I said.

"Sorry you don't get a hot dog stand," Emma said.

"That's all right," he said, putting his hands into the pockets of his dress pants. "You know, I hadn't been inside the bookmobile until last week. My mother asked me to go with her. And wouldn't you know, Mrs. Button found me the best book to read. I don't think I've read a book since college. I'd forgotten how nice it is to read something for fun." Just then, the music changed and got louder. He gave us a little wave. "I'll let you get back to the fun. No hard feelings, all right?"

"Okay," I said.

After he left, we looked at one another and smiled.

Emma grabbed our hands, swung them back and forth, and started singing along to the song. *"Shake it off, shake it off."*

Carmen, looking over our shoulders, said, "Hey, can I introduce you guys to someone?"

"Sure," Emma said.

"Follow me." She led us over to a table where her brother, Oscar, was sitting, next to a petite woman with her black hair twisted into a neat bun on the top of her head.

"This is my mother, Ana," Carmen said. "Mama, these are my friends Emma and Juliet."

Ana stood up and gently shook our hands and told us it was nice to finally meet us. "You should come to our home sometime. I can cook you some chiles rellenos. Carmen's favorite."

"Wow, we'd love that! Right, Juliet?" Emma said.

"For sure," I replied.

"Do you like the centerpieces we made, Mama?" Carmen asked, pointing to the one in the middle of her table. There were two old books stacked on top of each other and wrapped with a pretty white ribbon. On top of the books sat a small vanilla candle and two tulips in a crystal vase. It had been so fun to go to a used bookseller and buy a bunch of vintage hardcover books. We couldn't help but flip through them and read some of the poems and stories as we made the centerpieces. When I'd found the idea on the internet, I knew it'd be perfect. After all, it was the bookmobile that had brought Mr. Dooney and Ms. Strickland together. He'd gone to the senior center to ask about a room for the arts and crafts fair, he'd met Ms. Strickland, and the rest was history.

"Very pretty," Carmen's mom said. "Just like you, *mija*." She waved her hand at us. "All of you."

"Thanks," Emma and I said.

Just then, the DJ put on a song with a really good beat. Everyone flew to the dance floor and sang along with the lyrics. *"We are family."*

"We should dance," Emma said. She looked at Carmen's mom. "All of us. It'll be fun!"

I shook my head. "I don't really dance."

"What?" Emma took my hand, looked into my eyes, and smiled. "Juliet, come on. Please? We'll be right there with you."

How could I say no to that?

Carmen grabbed her mother's and brother's hands and gently pulled them toward the dance floor. We followed along, and when we got there, we formed a little circle. Before I knew what was happening, my body was moving to the beat. As we danced, Emma pointed her finger at each of us and sang along. *"We are family."*

I looked around at all the people who had come together to celebrate the love of two people. My heart felt big. Full. Happy.

Family isn't just who you live with. It's not just the people you're related to. It's the people who know you're scared of sharks and try to protect you from them. It's the people who say, "Come to my house anytime, you're always welcome here." It's the people who listen when you need to talk and make you laugh when you need it the most.

I couldn't make Carmen's wish come true—to have her dad back and both of her parents safe in the place they called home. But I could love her. Love them. Like family. Because aren't we all a part of the same large family, just trying to do the best we can?

I grabbed Ana's hands and held them in mine as we swung back and forth. She tilted her head back and laughed. I told myself to remember that moment and write about it in my notebook of beautiful things later. Because there was nothing, absolutely nothing, more beautiful than seeing her happy like that.

"*We are family,*" I sang to her.

I hoped she knew how much I meant it.

On a starry night, anything is possible . . .

Read on for a sneak peek of Juliet's
first adventures in Mission Beach!

Back in third grade, my teacher, Mrs. Arlington, called me "quirky" in my report card. To describe my personality. Mom said quirky isn't bad, it just means I like to do things differently. Like, when Mrs. Arlington gave us an assignment to write a letter to our hero, I wrote to my cat. Everyone else wrote to an athlete or a movie star or to a special family member. In my letter, I made a list of seven reasons why my cat was my hero. For example, when I first wake up, and Casper is asleep at the foot of my bed, he lets me pet his super-soft belly and it's the most comforting thing you could ever imagine.

I like lists; they make me feel good. But if I'd written to a movie star, I would have been lucky to come up with even one thing, much less a whole list.

Sometimes, though, I wonder if I'm too quirky. Or *unusual*—the word Mom uses when she talks about my art and lists. She says it's "unusual" that I love messy art projects as much as I love organizing everything into detailed lists. To me, that's like saying it's unusual if you like both cats *and* dogs. Why not both?

For some reason, I was thinking about that as I walked out the door and down a path that runs across one quiet street before landing at the boardwalk of Mission Beach. It was pretty crowded—lots of people walking, running, and riding bikes. At least our cottage wasn't super close to the amusement park. It's always packed down there. I crossed over into the sand, and as I looked out at the big, blue ocean, the warm sun on my face, I felt a little bit better about life in that moment. Maybe this wouldn't be so bad. Maybe I'd make some new friends right away. Maybe the three of us would get along just fine without Dad around.

Or maybe I was unusual *and* delusional. That was probably it.

I kicked off my flip-flops, picked them up, and walked toward the ocean in the coarse, hot sand. It was a clear March day with hardly a cloud in the sky. I took a deep breath of the salty air and sat down. A few feet ahead of me, closer to the water, a dark-haired girl who looked about my age and a younger boy were making a fancy sand castle with large turrets and a moat around it. The whole thing looked like something you'd see in a sand castle–building contest. I turned and watched a teen girl play Frisbee with her black Lab. She'd throw the Frisbee at him and he'd jump up and catch it. They did it over and over again. It was amazing.

Mom's phone vibrated in my pocket. I pulled it out to see what was happening. It was a text from Dad.

That child support amount is unacceptable. Come on, Wendy. Be reasonable.

I rolled my eyes as I clicked off the screen. *Please. Stop.*

The trip of a lifetime . . .

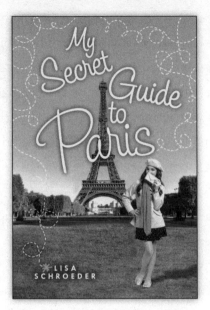

Nora loves everything about Paris, from the Eiffel Tower to *chocolat chaud*. Of course, she's never actually been there—she's only visited through her grandma Sylvia's stories. And just when they've finally planned a trip together, Grandma Sylvia is suddenly gone, taking Nora's dreams with her.

Nora is crushed. She misses her grandmother terribly, but she still wants to see the city they both loved. So when Nora finds letters and a Paris treasure map among her grandma Sylvia's things, she dares to dream again . . .

She's not sure what her grandma wants her to find, but Nora knows there are wonderful surprises waiting for her in Paris. And maybe, amongst the croissants and *macarons*, she'll even find a way to heal her broken heart.

A little piece of magic . . .

When Phoebe finds a beautiful antique at a flea market, she's not sure if it's as valuable as it looks. But inside she discovers something truly amazing—a letter, written during World War II, from a young girl to her sister who's been evacuated from London. The letter includes a "spell" for bringing people closer together: a list of clues leading all through the city. Each stop along the way adds up to magic.

Phoebe is stunned. Not only has she found a priceless piece of history, but the letter is exactly what she needs—she's also separated from her sister, though not by distance. Alice leaves for university soon, but in the meantime, she wants nothing to do with Phoebe. They used to be so close. Now that Phoebe has this magical list, maybe she can fix everything! That is, unless she accidentally makes everything worse instead . . .

Follow your heart . . .

Keys to the City

LISA SCHROEDER

Lindy can't wait for summer. Her family has moved to a beautiful old brownstone in New York City, where her parents are opening a bed-and-breakfast. She'll meet new people, visit her friends in Brooklyn, and spend lots of time curled up with a good book.

Or so she thought. Right before school ends, Lindy's class gets a summer assignment: to find their "true passion." Something they love *and* that they're good at. Something special. Their *thing*.

So much for a relaxing summer.

Then some new friends offer to help Lindy explore the city and go on adventures to find her passion. Lindy isn't sure it'll work, but New York is a big place. If the city can help Lindy unlock her potential, maybe the key to the perfect summer will be hers after all . . .